THE FOURTH MAN ON THE ROPE

Books by Evelyn Berckman

EVELYN BERCKMAN
THE FOURTH MAN ON THE ROPE

1972
DOUBLEDAY & COMPANY, INC., GARDEN CITY, NEW YORK

Library of Congress Catalog Card Number 74-175359
Copyright © 1972 by Evelyn Berckman
All Rights Reserved
Printed in the United States of America

With grateful and admiring thanks
to
All Archivists, Keepers and Librarians
on both sides of the water
who place at the public disposal their
untiring patience and courtesy
together with their accomplished help
Not forgetting my special joys
at the Old Brompton Road Branch

THE FOURTH MAN ON THE ROPE

I

Two women, young but not in their first youth, were walking along the sea-front. The dark sky under which they walked, the damp chill and a sullen wallowing sea all suggested winter, yet this was only mid-September—testimony to the freak reversal, since August, of the mild English Autumn—or not so much reversal as betrayal. Storms here and storms there along the coast, floods at Lewisham and elsewhere were part of this disrupted pattern; so was the tearing wind at their backs that pushed them along rather agreeably—except for the thought that on the way back they would be facing into it. Now, between three and four in the afternoon, heavy cloud was quenching the light as in November; the total desertion of the promenade underlined the seasonal death of a holiday area.

Through this unpropitious gloom the two women paced with the air of old friends, or at least familiars; the blonde and taller one seemed, when not actually talking, to lapse into what was either abstraction or a faint habitual reserve. Not so the other, obviously irked by the silences that now and again descended; she would glance restively at her companion and then, having visibly restrained herself once or twice, with an equally visible plunge would re-initiate conversation.

'I *do* hope you'll like it,' she said in obvious repetition, abruptly. 'I do *so* hope you'll like it, Bally.'

'I'm sure I shall,' said the other. Her tone and half-smile were acquiescent and inattentive.

'Well, but I mean—' said the first one '—having recommended it, I feel *responsible.*'

She spoke with habitual abruptness and over-emphasis; also in her attractive voice there survived, too subtly to be called lapses, some hallmarks of her origins. Not in the form of actual corruptions, and she had even conquered something more difficult—the characteristic inflections or rhythms of a racial lilt; yet here and there lingered betraying single vows from her very first moments of speech, too deep in her ever to be uprooted.

'I *do* feel responsible,' she was insisting.

'You needn't though,' murmured the one addressed as Bally.

'I needn't, but I do,' her companion returned, and had to conceal a sudden irritation. *My God, those clothes of yours*, she thought. *That pudding-basin hat.* 'Nothing's open by the end of September,' she continued aloud, 'but the big hotels, and they're—you know—twenty pounds a week at least. All the nice guest-houses are closed up too, and the ones still open are horrible. I went into all that thoroughly, Alison pet—when you wrote you were coming.'

'It was kind of you to go to all that trouble,' Alison murmured. 'Terribly kind, Myra.'

'No trouble—I wanted you to be comfortable,' Myra returned vigorously. 'But you don't know for how long you'll be here, actually—?'

'No.' Alison shook her head. 'Depends on how long the job will take.'

'Well, there you are, to be here a longish time and not be comfortable, it's no joke. That's why I risked booking you into my digs, in spite of a few misgivings.'

'Why misgivings?'

'Oh, I don't know! It's not everyone's cup of tea, a place like that—a bit seedy, a bit amateurish . . . but there *are* advantages,' she pressed on fervidly. 'Mrs. Mowbray's not the average grim landlady by a long chalk, she's—well, a saint—even though a colonel's widow.' She laughed disparagingly; her laugh was like her speech, abrupt, challenging, and a little too loud. 'And it's clean. And the food's very decent, considering the price. Once people get in there they stop forever, you bet. Because it's reasonable for nowadays, *frightfully* reasonable.'

'Yes, very,' agreed the other.

'And it's a small establishment, not a lot of decayed oldsters getting one down. Just six of us, including you,' Myra drove on. 'So I grabbed the chance when that old stringbean Miss Ravenshaw died at last. Not in your room,' she reassured hastily. 'In hospital.'

'Oh.'

'And thank God the place doesn't call itself Marvella or Ocean View or something ghastly like that, it has no name—it's just called Mowbray's.'

'I'm sure I'll do very well there,' returned her companion, and seemed to recall herself from vagueness by conscious effort. 'The big hotels would be completely beyond me, and your place sounds just what I'd like. So thank you for steering me into it, thank you very much, dear Myra,' she said warmly, and smiled.

The voluble Myra, for an instant, was stripped of volubility. Some quality of her friend's smile beyond her power of definition—the serenity in it, the composure, the thanks too-absent of gush—this complex bafflement renewed, then gave voice, to an earlier irritation.

'Alison,' she said abruptly. 'That getup of yours is too old for you, far too old.'

With palpable but mild surprise Alison turned upon her friend the same baffling smile, serene and undisturbed. 'I've got to buy stuff that lasts,' she deprecated, and glanced down at her utility camel's-hair coat and sensible shoes. 'I can't go chasing after every whim of fashion.'

'But you look like a—a mistress in a second-rate school or a sister in a nursing-home or something,' Myra complained. 'Because you've had one unsatisfactory marriage, you needn't dig your own grave and climb in.'

'I've no intention of digging my grave,' returned Alison. 'Whatever my marriage was, it gave me Chris. A boy like that makes up for—'

'Not for everything,' the other interrupted. 'Don't tell me everything, I shan't believe it.'

'He does make up for everything.' Again Alison smiled that smile—gentle, maddeningly impenetrable. 'He does, you know.'

'Rot. To think you could change like this, in ten years or so!' Myra despaired, with an old schoolmate's shattering frankness. '*Must* you spend every penny you have on Chris? *Must* you look as if you—as if you were out to *make* yourself old, deliberately—?'

'I'm not young, and I don't mind being dowdy,' murmured Alison, retreating visibly into her shell of aloofness. Myra, as visibly gathering her forces of rebuttal, checked all at once.

'Bally, look!' she hissed on a note of urgent, dramatic conspiracy. Her eyes were focussed intently on something distant, her tone and manner were half-gleeful, half-malicious. 'Look! do you see that woman?'

The light, dull but static, revealed as mere silhouette the only living creature beside themselves on the long vista stretching out deserted and wind-torn. There could

be no question of detail at this distance, but even so there
was something odd about it.

'D'you *see* her?' Myra repeated, agog with some inexplicable excitement.

'I see her,' Alison returned neutrally. 'I couldn't very
well miss her.' By common and unspoken consent they
fell silent and watched the person's approach—Alison
with an extra attentiveness caught from Myra's excitement and fixed concentration.

Coming toward them on the opposite side of the
promenade, bending into the relentless wind with an
opposition as unrelenting, was a figure that became progressively stranger, first as a walking beanpole bent at an
angle, then as a very old woman. Even by the unrevealing
light she was marked all over with the mark of the ec-
centric; as she came abreast of them her garments could
be seen blowing out behind her with the effect, if not the
actuality, of tatters. Even half-bowed as she was her unusual height was evident, also her excessive thinness; in
some arcane manner it was plain that upon a bony frame
she had piled layers and layers of shabby clothing, seemingly all black. The determination of her step and the
vigour with which she breasted the vicious swooping
gusts were remarkable. Without a glance in their direction, with no slackening in her grim progress she passed
on, grotesque and black against the background of dark
choppy sea.

'I'm glad,' said Myra, after the momentary silence the
apparition left in its wake. 'Glad we happened to meet
her. She's a pretty alarming bit of news to meet for the
first time, across a dinner-table.'

'You mean she . . . ?'

'*Yes*, dear, she lives at Mowbray's,' Myra confirmed
ironically. 'Oldest inhabitant I shouldn't wonder, and

thinks she's queen of the castle. And poor—so poor it isn't true.'

'Oh?'

'Hardly a bean to her name, I should say, just barely enough to scrape by. She's got some sort of arrangement with Caroline Mowbray, obviously—and I'll bet you Caroline doesn't make a penny out of it, but she plays along just the same. Now your average landlady wouldn't do that, but I told you Caroline wasn't average.'

'Who is this old lady?' Alison asked.

'Mrs. Lees-Milburn, and better not try shortening it to Milburn—she'll tear strips off you if you do. A relic, grisly but unique,' Myra stated with conviction. 'You won't meet *her* like again in a hurry, no fear.'

'How do you mean?'

'Well—' Myra launched herself with verve and appetite. 'She's immensely old, you saw—ninety or perhaps over. Her mother was by way of being a figure in her day, sort of a minor literary hostess of an intellectual salon and knew everyone, or almost—had these dreary gatherings of eminent Victorians with beards. The kind that're being unveiled today by frank biographies that couldn't be published earlier,' she added in aside. 'High Tennysonian and Carlylian thought, plus lifelong constipation and impotence.'

'I see.'

'You don't see,' Myra rebutted. 'You don't begin to see. The whole point is that all these sacred pundits corresponded with each other simply nonstop—passed their whole time writing six-page letters, apparently, God knows when they found time for their poetry and so forth. It was a period of enormous correspondences—*you* know.'

Alison nodded.

'Well!' Myra ascended triumphantly to her revelation. 'Well, the point is that this old monstrosity you've just seen, her mamma was one of the Browning circle and corresponded as madly as the best of them. And,' she wound up with a flourish, 'the hag has a trunk, literally a *trunkful* of letters, quite probably from every famous name of the period. The Brownings of course, but who couldn't be in there—George Eliot and her two little tame husbands, Ruskin, the Rossettis, Dickens—all that lot.'

A total silence ensued; on Alison's part slightly bemused, on Myra's deliberate, as if she were giving time for the news to sink in.

'With the enormous prices such things're making nowadays,' Alison hazarded at last, 'a collection of papers like that must be valuable.'

'*You*, a librarian, are telling *me*, another librarian? Well, really!'

'I wonder someone hasn't got wind of them,' Alison pursued, 'and tried to buy them.'

'Oh, she's had offers,' returned Myra. 'Certain circles know about the trunk's existence—academic and library and so forth. There's even a tale about some American professor who came down without warning or introduction of any kind—just burst into the lounge and hit her broadside with all that American matiness, you know— and the story is that this old scarecrow rose up in her rags and said, "I am *not* receiving you!" and swept out of the room. It might be true,' she appended consideringly. 'It sounds her style.'

'But why doesn't she sell them?' Alison queried reasonably, 'and live in comfort, instead of—'

'*Sell?* she sell?' Myra cut her off with burlesque horror.

'Sell her holy mamma's holy correspondence? She'd sooner starve.'

For another wordless interval Alison's imagination, irresistibly enchained, hovered about the unknown cache.

'Are they important?' she asked finally. 'The letters?'

'Who knows?' Myra retorted. 'When she won't let anyone examine them? Not anyone, period.'

'They've some value, whatever they are.' With professional pessimism, Alison canvassed poorer prospects. 'Even if the Browning letters are the later ones, when he lived in London and was always writing little notes to titled women, at the very least they're worth—'

'Bally! you *clever* thing!' Myra broke in. Her distended eyes and nostrils, her throbbing voice, telegraphed sudden drama. 'Bally, you've given me the most wonderful idea! *That's* how to do it! and I never before realized—' She broke off and began explaining rapidly. 'Supposing I throw cold water on the *importance* of her letters in front of everybody—hint they aren't anything in particular—mightn't that goad her into letting someone see them?' With mounting excitement she stared at Alison. 'I'll do it! I'll tackle her at dinner. And especially if you'll back me up—'

'I? I'll do nothing of the kind,' Alison put in, alarmed. 'Embroil myself like that, when I've hardly got here? Are you mad?'

'Oh, I shan't start anything tonight.' Myra was gleeful with possibility and impervious to rebuke. 'I'll choose my moment, no fear.'

'Just leave me out of it,' persisted Alison. 'Right out of it.'

On an excited giggle Myra subsided; it might be doubted that she had even heard her companion. At the end of a silence she digressed, 'So you've seen one sample, at least, of our funny little lot at Mowbray's.'

'Tell me about the others.' Too promptly perhaps, Alison seized on the change of subject. 'Three of them, you said? Who are they?'

'Well.' Myra was newly animated. 'There's rather a charming old boy, a Major James Grant—Jimmy. Retired of course, and simply lives for golf, chess and bridge. Still personable—' it escaped being *pairsonable* by a hair's-breadth '—like lots of those Army types.' She bridled a bit, self-consciously. 'I'm playing a partnership with him tonight, actually—there're some little bridge-clubs hereabouts.' She turned on Alison her bright avid glance. 'D'you play bridge?'

'Goodness no.'

'I thought not—I don't remember you as a card-type, one is or one isn't.—Let's go as far as that next groyne and turn back,' she decreed, with one of her swooping changes of subject. 'We'll be back just in time for tea—I've ordered for both of us.'

'A cup of tea will be lovely,' Alison admitted. 'After this wind.'

'Teas are extra you know, Caroline—Mrs. Mowbray—can't help herself on that. But today,' Myra flourished handsomely, 'you're my guest.'

'Oh no, no, you mustn't—'

'Shut up, Bally, you've just come. It's a celebration.'

'Well, it's very kind of you,' said Alison, somehow without pleasure. 'Thank you very much.'

'*My* pleasuah, I'm suah,' Myra derided.

Silent again they continued toward the groyne, a line of black irregular teeth crunching their way out to sea. It was Myra who broke the pause by asking abruptly, 'Did you ever hear the expression, *the fourth man on the rope?*'

'Why—' Alison, with an effort, roused herself from the interval of peace; only now, when it was ruptured, did she realize her degree of relief from Myra's incessant and demanding voice. '—why no. The fourth man on the rope?' she echoed. 'No, I don't think I've heard it.'

'Never? it doesn't convey anything to you?'

'No, not a thing.'

'Well, it's rather a horrible expression.' But her accent was rather gloating than of distaste. 'It's climbers' language, actually—the sort of fools that crawl up a hideous rocky sheer a thousand feet high, *brrrr!* Well, they're roped together by threes, did you know—?'

'No, I didn't.'

'Well, they are. And if the rope breaks and kills one or all of them, there's a saying—that the fourth man did it— the fourth man on the rope.'

'But you just said, didn't you, there were only three men on the rope—?'

'Aha, that's just it!' Myra triumphed. 'There *is* no fourth man, don't you see?'

'Well, I . . . begin to see.'

'Of *course* you do! The Fourth Man's the breaking-point in the rope—and he's been with them all the time.' Her eyes and teeth gleamed smiling through the dusk. 'And they never knew.'

'Yes, of course. It *is* rather a ghastly expression, isn't it?'

'Now take a person—like you, for instance.' Myra was speaking faster, impelled by some headlong urgency. 'Someone so utterly calm and composed—' The look she flashed at Alison was like malice peering around a corner, a face too-quickly withdrawn. 'I love to look at all that calm and think, "Now what would crack *you* wide open, I wonder?" It's fun, rather,' Myra rattled on, 'to look at people from that point of view—look at those nice smug fronts and wonder what would break them up completely.'

'Good heavens.' Alison, thoroughly startled, turned wide eyes on her companion. 'You collect breaking-points, do you? Is that what you mean?'

'Well—' Myra giggled, an excited sound with an undertone of slyness '—one might call it that.'

'What a hobby,' commented the other. 'Not pleasant, if I may say so.'

'Everyone's got a Fourth Man, you know.' Myra was undeterred by criticism. 'What's your Fourth Man, Bally?'

'Myra, really!'

'You won't say,' Myra accused, more than ever gleeful. 'You're afraid, perhaps? or maybe you don't even know, yourself?' She cocked her head in a birdlike style that matched her elfin size and staccato movements. 'I'll have to guess.'

'Please don't,' Alison said with unintended sharpness.

'With you—' Myra ignored the prohibition, speaking in a tone between judicial and mischievous '—with you, the breaking-point would be . . . let's see now. . . .'

'Myra,' expostulated the object of diagnosis. 'Why do you insist on going on with this, when you know I don't like it?'

'You don't like it? Aha!' Triumph suffused Myra again. 'That's an admission, you know. All right, *be* unhelpful,' she adjured. 'I'll find out your Fourth Man, I usually do. And add him,' she concluded, 'to my collection.'

'A nasty collection, rather.' Alison herself hardly realized her split-second substitution for *dangerous*. 'Decidedly nasty.'

'Oh, I don't know, one amuses one's self as one can.' Myra's tone, negligent all at once, indicated her abandonment of the topic. 'Come on, let's turn back.'

A silence fell; they needed all their breath as they faced into a ceaseless buffeting that made Alison clutch her hat and whipped strands of dark wavy hair from under Myra's head-scarf. Alison, during this silence, glanced once at her companion and glanced away. The degree of relief she experienced at the present cessation of the other's chattering was in abeyance, this time, to discomfort—a curious sort of unease in which old accustomed recognitions were brought up short against unfamiliar barriers. A long college friendship entitled her to think she knew Myra well, even very well; still possessed by memories of a girl, before this woman she groped in bafflement for some surviving strand of identity. This new Myra, full of hungry curiosities and pryings into the legitimate reserves of others: unhealthy, indecent. . . . And with this spiritual change for the worse, almost she could fancy a physical change keeping pace; the girl's grace of the young Myra malignly transformed into a small insectile grace—something poisonous that darts in, stings, darts out again. . . . People change, she thought not very originally, and in fairness wondered if the changes in herself were equally off-putting to Myra. Ten years with no contact but occasional letters; ten years, a long time. . . .

As soon as they turned off the front their ears were unstuffed of roaring wind and sea and their limbs eased and lightened.

'Funny,' Myra said, utilizing the lull at once. 'Funny, your coming to work in the library where I'm working.'

'Yes,' concurred the other, still bemused with time and change.

'Still, it's unhandy—your not knowing for how long.'

'He didn't say—Mr. Durant didn't say.'

'Well,' Myra shrugged.

'The quiet,' Alison said all at once, and halted in the village street. 'The *quiet*—!'

'Ah! you've noticed.'

'But why hasn't this place been ruined?' Alison demanded, with dire memories of beauty irretrievably savaged. 'Why isn't it a dormitory for Folkestone or somewhere?'

'Because,' said Myra on an enigmatic note, 'Lord Gurney of Allhayes owns the whole damned village of Beechen Hayes, that's why. Buys up everything that comes on the market—won't let in shops or developers or anything.'

'Cheers for Lord Gurney,' murmured Alison.

'Well, I don't know.' Myra was snappish. 'I don't like mummified gentry that hold up progress with money they've never earned. Still,' she conceded, 'it's postcard-pretty, I expect. And our library—1703. Correctly infested,' she mocked, 'with death-watch beetle and a waxwork board of Governors. You'll adore all that quaintness, a little Conservative like you.'

'I'm sure I shall,' Alison agreed, ignoring derision.

'Also, if you please—' Myra abandoned criticism and derogation; her tone was now serious if not a trifle pompous. 'Champernowne's not a public library you know, its private—an endowed library.'

'Yes, your Mr. Durant mentioned that in one of his letters.'

'Ah yes.' On a barely-perceptible pause, Myra's voice took on an unfamiliar note. 'D'you know him well?'

'I don't know him at all,' Alison murmured inattentively; her mind was running on something else. 'We've only corresponded.'

'Oh. Well then, I'd better tell you. He's—'

'Myra.' Unhearing and abrupt, Alison opposed a counter-impetus to Myra's; the mysterious unknown trove still possessed her. 'Myra, that old woman with the letters—she knows what's in them, doesn't she?'

'She knows as much,' Myra retorted, 'as a fish on a slab. She's county—gentry—all that muck. I've heard her call Browning "that poet-fella," believe it or not. And I'll bet you anything,' she challenged, 'that she's never read even one of the letters. All she knows is, they're family papers—just part of her ancestor-worship, like all that type. The hell with her, you'll meet her soon enough.— Now about our Mr. Durant.' She halted abruptly in mid-pavement, within feet of their boarding-house. 'Prepare yourself, Bally. He's at Mowbray's too, I fear—along with us 'umble ones.'

'Oh.' Alison groped briefly. 'You mean he lives there?'

'Heavens no! the head of Champernowne *live* there? No, he's only stopping for the moment. Even so it's a bit constraining, having one's boss in the same house, but it can't be helped. So I thought,' she concluded, 'I'd better warn you.'

'But. . . .' Alison's puzzlement was more from Myra's air of intense and secret meaning than from any excess of interest. '—I mean, hasn't he a home? Isn't he married?'

'Oh, he's married all right,' the other returned cryptically. 'That's his trouble.—Oh Lord!' A glance at her wrist dispersed her next utterance, whatever it was. 'No time, I'll tell you later—*alone*.' Suddenly she took Alison's arm and squeezed it with affection. 'Oh Bally, I *am* glad you're here, it's like old times. Come on, let's trundle in now, or no tea.'

Her bedroom was soothing in its quiet, soothing in its very plainness and dulness. She was going to like this place, she thought as she unpacked; as Myra had said, it managed somehow to avoid the atmosphere of guest-house, offering here and there small bright evidences of the family stronghold it once had been. One of these souvenirs had so pleased her, from the moment of seeing it, that after freshening for dinner she lingered in order to review and enjoy it in detail. This was nothing more than the upper hall, on which opened the six bedrooms and two bathrooms. A rectangle far more spacious than many rooms, it had an extraordinarily well-kept look. On its polished floor-boards lay a thin faded Oriental, once a very good one; against one wall stood a handsome grandfather clock, its old heart beating steadily, and against the other a card-table holding a set of three orna-ments. To this group, that had drawn her attention from the first, she crossed over, noting that the table was un-doubtedly late Georgian and that its polished mahogany leaf, open against the wall, was excellent background for the pieces ranged before it—a lamp flanked by two matching vases with frilled lips, all in a shade of purest sky-blue, faintly opalescent. She picked up one of the vases and put it down again, surprised at its weight. Early Victorian, she would judge, and though no devotee of opaline glass of any period she knew that a set like this—not a crack nor chip anywhere in it—would cost between forty and fifty pounds in any antique shop. All so pleas-ing, so harmonious by the dim mellow light of the lamp. . . . . .

Below her an indefinite musical roar broke out and mounted; she obeyed the summons, going downstairs with the gentle picture of old cherished wood and lustrous glass somehow imprinted in her mind as symbols of a happy domestic peace that must once, in that bygone day, have seemed secure and solid as rock.

II

Sitting in the lounge after dinner, blessedly alone for the moment, she stirred and stirred her coffee-cup absently, looking into its depths as if she could find there a quantity of useful information. What she felt, actually, was peace—a peaceful confirmation of Myra's feeling about Mowbray's, and her peaceful experience of it so far. This lounge, its semi-shabbiness redeemed by its informality and friendly atmosphere . . . an enormous dog of indefinable ancestry had wandered in during tea and begged biscuits, taking her welcome for granted; a dog obviously cherished though excessively pregnant . . . yes, there was kindness in the air, intelligence too somehow, a feeling of home. Also the food was as Myra had described it, plain but adequate. Excellence and lavishness were hardly to be expected at the price; enough that one rose from table not resentful of skimpiness nor menaced by a stomach nursing its first revenges for what had been put into it.

Against the food passing muster, there was of course to be considered her intense dislike of communal dining. Still, the table was spacious, too large actually for six people; no risk there of alien elbows or being crowded against someone antipathetic to you, for good or bad reasons. Balancing her spoon on the edge of the cup, unseeingly watching drops collect on its edge and fall back into the coffee, she gave herself to an assessment of her fellows under this roof. Foolish to attempt judgments on four unknown entities at first encounter, yet she continued pursuing the project and calling up the various images in turn. . . . .

First, Mrs. Lees-Milburn; the grotesque silhouette fighting the wind earlier on, now filling in its outlines with details of her own tone and manner. A fierce, assured and arrogant old relic of days when women like herself had sowed, in terrains colonial and otherwise, a durable hatred of the English, clearly she had lived all her life in terms of big houses and eight or ten servants, and had never got over it. In her present reduced circumstances she seemed to derive her chief satisfaction from dominating her table-mates—or thinking she dominated them—and from seeing that one of them, at least, shrivelled gratifyingly in her presence. As for the Major Grant that Myra had mentioned, the chess and bridge addict, he seemed to her a stereotype of the retired military man with his upright commanding carriage, his gentlemanly look and manner, indelible stamp of an ancient prestige; she was glad that Myra had such a nice playmate.

In fact all the puzzle and mystery of the table, if any, seemed to converge in a single person, one Mr. Marx or Marcus. Idly yet persistently she kept trying to fit him into his present surroundings; persistently, because she could hardly imagine how he had got in at all. An unprepossessing little man and obviously the chief casualty of the Lees-Milburn manner, he sat with obvious discomfort and apologetic politeness in the cruel, well-bred exclusion of the dinner-table; hesitantly offering from time to time a timid smile or a remark either ignored or answered by a drawled *Oh?* of insulting irrelevance. The spectacle was so painful to Alison that she was driven, at last, to pretend he was not there; if she had been sitting next to him certainly she would have conversed, she assured herself, then from mere discomfort of memory fled Mr. Marcus or at least put him aside.

After this she sat half-dreaming, in a strange and unaccustomed frame of mind; wanting to give herself to the thought of the one remaining person at table, yet hesitating exactly like a weak swimmer before water of unknown depth. How many years since she had thought in this way of a man, or—more accurately—how many years since she had seen a man she wanted to think about. . . . .

Her first unwilled and hesitant trial of the water was forcibly postponed by the entrance of Myra—Myra attractively made-up and furbished, carrying a coat over her arm.

'Now!' she ejaculated without preamble, swooping upon a chair and drawing it up close, then lowering her voice and speaking fast. 'About Tom Durant—he's here either because his wife threw him out or he walked out, no one knows exactly. That's why he's holed up at Mrs. Mowbray's—she's a cousin of his, actually. They're both local, everyone's related to everyone else hereabouts.'

She paused for breath, giving Alison a chance to remark, 'I'd expect him to stop somewhere a little more grand, wouldn't you?'

'That's just it!' Myra hissed, looking sharply at the door, and plunged on. 'He's pretty well paid, I expect, but not well enough to keep his wife in their flat and do himself very luxuriously on his own.'

'Oh,' Alison murmured, blank with too much novelty to digest all at once.

'And this bitch of a wife, she comes to the library and plays him up. The *library!*' she declaimed. 'Invades his

office and makes scenes. Well, you can imagine how he
loves that. Just a little too much of it, enough to break
surface, and he's a damned good chance of losing his
job.'

'I—I can see that. He's got rather a special reputation,
though? He's supposed to have put the library on the
map—?'

'Oh, he has done, absolutely! he's *dedicated* to Champernowne. But all the same anything actually scandalous
—noisy—they'd never tolerate it, our board of Governors.
—Lord Gurney's one of them, by the way. I told you,' she
digressed scornfully, 'we're a stinking little pocket of
county hereabouts. All those retired generals and admi-
rals on our board—that sort of fungus—what they say,
goes.'

'I see,' responded the other.

'Well, that's how it is. This female hyena can torment
a man like that, perhaps ruin him, and what's he to do,
aside from murder? Of course,' she detailed regretfully,
'practically nothing of the row gets through to the
reading-room, except the occasional high-pitched note.
Our doors and walls, *solid!*— Now Durant's secretary,
Carew, she hears it all I bet, her room's next to his—but
try getting any value out of her. Loyal and close-mouthed,'
Myra snarled. 'Old sour-guts.'

'Tell me.' Alison, with a sense of being drawn into the
net of someone else's prejudices, tried to escape. 'Who
was that peculiar little man at dinner, that Mr. Marcus?'

'*He!* well may you ask.' On a note of new and recharged
denigration, Myra glanced at the door again and continued rapidly. 'How Caroline Mowbray ever let a type
like that into this place at all, I don't understand—no one
understands. She must have had an attack of Christianity,

or someone gave him a pretty compelling introduction, or something.'

'Why, Myra,' Alison taunted gently. 'Is that you speaking? Everyone's as good as everyone else, aren't they?'

'I've *never* said that,' with quick and characteristic fury Myra threw the charge back at her. 'Never!'

'Isn't prejudice the unforgivable thing?' Alison pursued unwisely. 'Or have I misunderstood you all these years?'

'Even a slum type like me,' Myra lashed out, 'can have preferences—!'

'Sorry, sorry.' With unqualified cowardice, Alison backed down; she had forgotten the potential dangers of such a gambit, while knowing that Myra's radicalism rested on intensely personal foundations. 'I was just joking.'

'Glad to hear it.' Yet a retreating animus denoted, in Myra, an equal unwillingness to pursue hostilities. 'But this greasy little object, at least he keeps himself to himself and nobody talks to him, so it's all right.—Bally!' she implored with sudden drama. 'Were you thinking of leaving, because of him? *Don't*, please don't, it's such fun for me, having you here. One hardly knows he's about, I promise you—don't let him put you off, Bally, please don't.'

'He doesn't put me off at all,' Alison demurred. 'I felt rather sorry for him.'

'Well, what's he expect, pushing in where he doesn't belong?' Myra followed another cautionary look toward the door with a glance at her wrist. 'Sweetie, I hate leaving you all on your own, your first evening here.'

'I'm loving it,' Alison smiled. 'So restful. But they don't seem to use the lounge very much in the evening, do they?'

'Well actually no, they don't. The great Durant, never. Jimmy Grant occasionally, but he doesn't talk, just reads his paper. The Marcus type knows better than to show his face in here, and a good thing too. Only—' Myra checked in the act of rising '—I'd better warn you about Lees-Milburn.'

'Why?'

'She *infests* the lounge, that's why—takes over entirely, till bed-time. She'd have been here before, but she always goes to the loo after dinner. So better get to hell out if you don't want her to catch you—or if she does,' she amended, 'just walk out on her, don't waste polite-ness on the old hag— Ah, Jimmy!' With remarkable speed —as the door opened on the Major's face of polite en-quiry—her voice changed from venomous to lilting. 'Com-ing, coming, just having an old-girls' natter.' She swept up her coat, only pausing to hiss, 'Remember now!'

The door closed upon them, restoring the silence; be-neath the overhead light that made the lounge seem bleaker by evening than by day, she continued to sit motionless for all Myra's warning. Relegating or ignoring the threat of Mrs. Lees-Milburn, with a faint unconscious smile and remote eyes she tried to recapture what Myra's entrance had dispelled: the dreaming interlude, the sweet painful compulsion that had gripped her from the first moment at table. . . . . .

Letters had preceded her coming to Champernowne, similar to other letters engaging her as a free-lance archivist; to the extent that she had thought of it at all, she had evolved from this correspondence the picture of other keepers and archivists well-known to her, among whom existed a certain similarity of type. Therefore, expecting a middle-aged or elderly man, she had been totally unprepared for the person she would meet tomorrow as her employer, whose silent bow—unsmiling—had followed Myra's fulsome introduction. All during dinner in fact, and as often as possible without attracting notice, her glance had been drawn to him. He could not be more than forty; his head was excellent, his features strikingly handsome. Not self-consciously in the way of some men, this handsomeness, not that way at all; in it was such breadth of intelligence, such strength combined with kindness, that the mere good looks were least part of the compelling charm and intense attractiveness of such a face. With all this went a strong and well-proportioned body; she had thought, *Anyone could be in love with him, anyone,* yet had wondered increasingly at his air of reserve, from which he seemed to exempt Mrs. Lees-Milburn alone. A way of distinguishing his only social equal, among them all? Off-putting if true . . . her wonderment had become resentful and finally apprehensive; he looked like being a snob, and snobs in her experience were difficult to work for. Misgiving began to touch her, more and more coldly . . .

Now, with Myra's revelations, she wondered at his manner no longer; easy enough to define the Fourth Man (horrid expression) that was riding his neck. His reserve that she had taken for pompousness she now saw as resignation and endurance, a fatalism that wrapped him like fog and blurred, to a certain degree, his impact of personality. And a man like this, it seemed, could be at the mercy of a termagant who invaded his office with rows and screaming tempers. . . . Too many such episodes and his superiors must get rid of him, however regretfully; Myra had been quite right, his wife could impede his career, even destroy it. . . . .

The door opened brusquely to admit the tall black apparition of the front, which directed itself toward her as inexorably as fate. Her apparel still suggested layer upon layer of draperies, and her disposition of these coverings as she sat down was reminiscent of a vulture alighting and unhurriedly furling its wide pinions as it decided which part of its meal to attack. Yet the presumptive victim, who had assumed a bland amiable look as the best defence against inquisition, found herself totally dislodged from her prepared position by the first dig of the curved beak.

'Your *friend*,' said the old woman with derogatory emphasis, and in a harsh assured voice, 'dresses *very* well.'

Mere surprise held the other silent a moment, so utterly unexpected was this opening gambit. That the words were loaded with insinuation was plain to the meanest intelligence, but what sort of insinuation was impossible to judge this early. As unreadiness prolonged her state of being at a loss, the vulture had repeated, 'Very well indeed.' She regarded her companion with a restrained, amused balefulness. 'Don't you think she dresses well?'

'I—I hadn't noticed,' Alison managed at last.

'Hadn't noticed! not that coat she wore, when the two of you were out walking on the front?'

So the violent wind and her battle against it—for all her appearance of not giving them a glance—had not prevented her sizing them up in detail; it was easy to believe that very little got past her.

'And that dress she was wearing just now,' the assault continued. 'Her dress, you didn't notice—?'

'Not particularly.'

'Well!' The old woman shrugged. 'Perhaps you wouldn't.' Her eyes summed up and dismissed Alison's useful crepe, dark brown. 'There *are* women, of course, with no dress sense at all.—Your name's Pendle?'

'Pendrell.'

'Welsh,' said Mrs. Lees-Milburn—not sufficiently interested, Alison conjectured, to be disparaging. 'But very far back, I'd imagine.'

'Yes.'

'Your *friend's* been saying you're going to work at Champernowne?' The inquisitor continued to underline *friend* invisibly. 'You're a librarian too, like your friend?'

'Yes.' Alison, in fact, was finding in herself a curiously-divided attitude; her instinct to repel the other's attack was constantly blunted by her feeling that the attack had some special and devious purpose, and by her wish to divine what this mysterious purpose was. Her state of ambivalence was cut short, actually, by the attacker's sudden loss of interest in the library.

'That dress your friend just had on,' she shot at Alison without preamble, and the mystery was solved. The light in her eyes was renewed, the malice in her face rekindled; she wanted to talk about Myra—by way of disparagement and denigration, obviously. Her whole aspect, that went dull and flat when she was bored, came to life at mention of Myra. Just why this relic should harbour so vivid an antagonism against a woman at least sixty years her junior, was mysterious in itself; one might suppose that mere inequality of age would exclude hatred—for unmistakably this flourishing rankness was hatred, and not something of lesser degree.

'A dress like that,' she was saying, 'one couldn't buy for less than fifty pounds, at the very least. And that blue coat of hers—ninety or a hundred pounds if it cost a penny.'

Between incredulity and bewilderment, Alison was silent.

'She's never worn good clothes here before,' the raucous old voice pursued. 'Poor, if anything. Well, not poor exactly, but very inexpensive—dowdy or at least careless. And then suddenly to blossom out like that! How can she afford it, a librarian? The answer's obvious, of course.' She smiled with vivifying malice. 'She's taken her little savings and bought a few fine feathers. Enticement of course—someone in her sights. Target's pretty obvious too, there aren't all that many. He'd better look sharp, poor old Jimmy Grant. Or else—' a deeper malignity etched her smile '—if it's not her savings she's spent, I can't believe that she's come by that much money honestly. And I'd never believe it was private or inherited money, not for a moment—people of her class don't inherit.'

A deeper stupefaction at the foolhardiness of it—the sheer recklessness—gripped Alison more completely. *Mrs. Lees-Milburn, did you ever hear of libel?* formed itself on her lips. *Supposing I repeated to Myra exactly what you've said?*

Instead, she broke from her paralysis and got up. 'I've had a hard day,' she said in a curt voice, 'so I'll say goodnight,' and walked out of the room.

Climbing the stairs, she was accompanied by a vision of Mrs. Lees-Milburn as the central occupant of a dusty web garnished with dead flies. And let her recognize this abrupt departure for the snub that it was; it would do her all the good in the world.

Upstairs she discovered that freeing herself from the old woman's presence was no simple matter, as if the stronger nature—even on so brief contact—had stamped itself on her more yielding one. With undesired clarity she heard the harsh voice, with undesired vividness saw the tallness, the big bony frame, the upright posture and commanding movements, not at all enfeebled. Her only concessions to nearly a century of existence were the texture of her face, crumpled parchment, and her extremely sunken eyes that had lost all trace of original blue or brown and were now reminiscent of standing peat-ater. A musty smell exhaled from her, either of old body-smell or of old dresses exhumed from God knows what unaired layers in old trunks or presses. But apart from these hallmarks of age there was nothing wrong with her faculties nor with her total awareness of the modern world; even in her backwater of life and time she retained a lively fashion-sense, she knew good clothes and she knew what was being worn. . . . The thought of clothes and her strictures on Myra made Alison pause in her dressing, then for a moment stop dead.

Having renounced smartness for herself, she cultivated (perhaps too strenuously?) an obliviousness of dress; now, with her pantihose halfway down her legs she sat trying to visualize what, actually, Myra had had on . . . ? It came back with suspicious readiness: a lovely sports-coat, thick soft wool in a subtle weave and colour never found in anything cheap. Then before going out, on her final appearance in the lounge . . . ? Yes, something in a blue-and-white wool, yet patently for evening: one of the new semi-dress woollens . . . both, as the old woman had said, expensive. And whose affair but Myra's after all, and who cared anyway?

With sudden temper she whipped her hobbled legs free of pantihose and her mind free of Mrs. Lees-Milburn, simultaneously. While unhooking her brassiere she tried hard to recapture that face across the dinner-table and the mood it evoked in her; the half-dreaming trance, soft and happy for no reason . . . . . useless; the harpy downstairs had torn the spell apart with its beak and claws. She finished undressing and stood up, having first let the room attain a semi-tropical warmth; the extra shillings in the meter had been her defence against her sudden longing for Chris, and against the homeless wail-ing of the wind outside. Her mirrored act of reaching for her night-gown drew her attention; she checked a moment, half-startled at her reflected nakedness, shapely and brilliantly blonde. Then with no warning she re-sponded to the sight with an unwilled, fathomless hatred and self-contempt.

'My body,' she addressed her image aloud. 'My celibate body.'

She thrust on her flannel night-dress as vengefully as if it were a hair-shirt, then put out the light and went to bed.

III

Buildings like the Champernowne still existed in England if one went far enough from Sussex, Surrey and Kent where an imbecile officialdom—sturdily committed to the tradition by which the English were always their own vandals—might seal living fields beneath asphalt and destroy irreplaceable beauty with fast motorways and stinking air. This far away however an old magic still, for a little time at least, stood unravaged. The Champernowne Library was housed in its original Regency building with a splendid curving facade and ranks of engaged columns; its dark look on this sunless chilly day was due (she felt) to its need for cleaning. Alison passed through its doors and into a familiar smell of aged buildings, unconquerable by any means employed against it; her nose twitched to a reminiscence of Mrs. Lees-Milburn's musty old smell. The entrance-hall was gloomily magnificent, a large oval paved in black and white marble, and set about with niches. Each contained a bust or statue, and she promised herself a detailed examination of them when she could; a seventeenth century endowment like this must be stuffed with objects of unknown value, the sort of thing for which auction-room dealers fought to pay astronomical prices; already she had got the impression of original Roubiliacs. . . . .

Massive mahogany doors flung wide beneath a grand looming doorcase of black marble opened into the general reading-room; Champernowne, essentially a research library, also served its village and surrounding area as a lending library. A few elderly men and women were already sitting and reading or drifting along the bookshelves; three women were on duty at the desk. One of them was Myra, going over a stack of returns.

'I hope,' she gritted between her teeth as Alison came alongside, 'I only hope there's a special hell reserved for people who put hairs in books as place-markers. Of all the *obscene* habits—!' She freed her fingers of a white one, long and clinging. 'And look at that!' With equal fury she displayed a vandalized page. 'You get some old fool with a maggot in his head about some point of grammar or something, and he'll deface the whole book with his corrections and marginal observations. I'd bar them from library privilege forever after if we could catch them, but we never can—' she broke off and glanced at the gargantuan clock, a show-piece in its own right. 'Will you be coming in every morning this late?'

'Goodness no,' Alison deprecated, not missing the implied criticism. 'Mr. Durant said not till ten-thirty, just today—he wouldn't be free to tell me about the job till then.'

'Oh.—Is that what he was saying to you, after breakfast?'

'Yes.' Even her momentary exchange with her employer had not escaped Myra, she thought, and felt a stir of annoyance—however undeveloped—at this unrelenting observation.

'Well, it's just on ten-thirty now. Over there.' Myra indicated. 'His secretary's the first door on the right, then his. Go on along, the watch-dog'll announce you. If it shows its teeth, never mind.'

Obscurely aware that Myra returned to winnowing books with increased bad temper, she followed directions through a door marked PRIVATE and into a corridor with plastic tiles underfoot.

'Yes, Miss Pendrell, go in please—Mr. Durant's expecting you.' Miss Carew was somewhere in the acrid fifties, with a calcified and dedicated neatness like the member of some conventual Order; the Order of St. Thomas Durant, Alison had no doubt. Even during the few steps between this office and the next she had a perception of the female jealousy and devotion, all the more violent for being tacit, that must swirl about this attractive man; at his threshold she sighed rather than smiled at the duplications—the stark repetitive poverty—of human patterns. And she herself, as recently as last night, had been on the verge of adding her bit to this emotional stew. . . . *Only on the verge*, she absolved herself as she put her hand on the doorknob, *and never again if I know it*.

'Good-morning again, Miss Pendrell,' he greeted her, rising. 'Sorry for this delay. Would you care for a short tour of the Champernowne first, before we talk about your job?'

Even knowing the special reputation of this place, in a world of historians and other specialists, she found the 'short tour' an eye-opener. The stacks, reaching forever into the bowels of the earth and crammed with the accumulations of two and a half centuries; a superb reference room, brilliantly lighted; a manuscript room of endless treasures, an unequalled repository of local history, seventeenth and eighteenth century, of this Kentish coast that had known such cruel defencelessness

and tumultuous fears, such forgotten daily heroisms. Upstairs was a small museum with fascinating cross-sections
of life in every social grade, from the rural labourer's im-
plements and his treen to the gentry's engraved wine-
glasses and table-silver and their children's lavish
doll-houses; a scene in wonderful waxwork of smugglers
fighting Revenue men was mounted flamboyantly among
the intercepted booty—brandy- and tobacco-casks and
scattered laces. Yet all this perfection of display and
maintenance she felt as having its source in the man beside her; his knowledge of its intricacies equalled by his
passion for all its aspects, a passion that brought his face
alive as he talked. Rare in her experience to find a man
so totally dedicated to antiquarianism, yet not the least
trace in him of scholarly dryness. . . . . .

'And now,' he said as they regained his office, 'we'll
get down to it, shall we? Without wasting any more of
your time?' He was unlocking a desk drawer from which
he produced a monster brass key, an original, and repeated the unlocking process on a door behind the desk.
Then she was obeying his gesture and going before him
to the inner room beneath its cold blaze of neon light,
then stopping dead with rather more consternation than
astonishment.

'Good Lord,' she murmured after a pause.
'Quite,' he returned. For a moment their united survey
moved over the massive disorder, the knee-deep welter
of a paper sea frozen in stormy movement. Papers covered the floor completely with hardly an inch to move,
papers loosely stacked or in tottering congeries of
bundles tied with tape; here and there stood toppling
brown pillars of books, scuffed and faded. Off these de-

posits came two familiar accents of bygones, a stifling
smell of dust and the breath of mouldy paper and bind-
ings; Alison estimated that the latest additions to the
mass might have been made well over a hundred years
ago. In the course of her work she had seen more than
one neglected muniment-room *in situ*, with contents
barbarously dumped out after the death of some final
survivor; she was used to monster accumulations of centuries, so distractingly unsorted that one hardly knew
where to begin; but this present chaos held its own with
anything she had so far encountered, and its having been
moved from its own location and piled here helter-skelter
was not going to simplify her task.

'Couldn't they have left it where it was?' she sighed.
'Long enough for someone to put it in rough order, before
bringing it here?'

'My dear Miss Pendrell,' he countered with wry
amusement. 'The house and the estate were bought before old Miss Tollemache was cold, in a manner of speaking, and we were given just so much time and no more
to salvage our bequest. The demolition crew was practically snapping at our heels as we brought the last of it
out, and our van wasn't welcome among the assorted
bulldozers and concrete-mixers, I assure you. Lovely late
Georgian country place it was, Tollemache House,' he
murmured. 'Neglected and going to ruin, but the old
lady clung to it. Lovely old gardens—peaceful.'

'Well, what of it?' she returned. 'Don't you know the
English have always been their own vandals? Don't you
know they've always destroyed the best of what they've
created, from kings to cathedrals? And don't you know
the destroyers outnumber the preservers in the end,
every time?'

'You feel strongly about it,' he observed.

'I don't feel strongly about anything.' In her face she felt the warmth of her little peroration; this flushing always annoyed her because, with her complexion, it was embarrassingly conspicuous. 'And if one does, it's a waste of time.—Now about this.'

She gestured toward the room, slightly embarrassed at her digression.

'I wasn't quite prepared for anything on this scale,' she pursued. 'And in view of what I see, I'm afraid I can't commit myself to a definite period of time. I'm sorry,' she apologized, 'but I couldn't limit myself, I couldn't possibly. Not that I'd anticipate anything very exciting in this lot, but one has to go slowly all the same—and how long it'll take God knows. So,' she concluded, 'if you'd like to change your mind about engaging me, I'd feel you were quite within your rights.'

'I'm quite aware of my rights,' he returned. 'Also I'd distrust anyone who offered to scramble through these thousands of papers within a specified time. So if it's agreeable to you, Miss Pendrell, our arrangement will stand—that is, if the terms proposed are satisfactory—?'

'Quite satisfactory,' she returned. The ironic coolness with which he had refused her offer had rubbed her the wrong way to a surprising degree; as her first unpleasant impression of pomposity returned, she felt combative and anxious to pay him back in his own coin.

'I hope everything's here that you'll need.' He indicated supplies plentifully laid on.

'I expect so, thank you,' she returned in a voice designed to make him feel snubbed, in case he had missed her first attempt.

'And one more thing, very important.' He paused briefly. 'As you see, the only access to this room is through

my office. Please let me beg you, Miss Pendrell,' he bore
on with peculiar urgency, 'when you have occasion to
absent yourself, even for a few moments, not to forget to
lock the door behind you. Please, never forget,' he repeated emphatically. 'I'm not always at my desk by any
manner of means, and I rely on you to see that no one's
admitted to this room but you and myself.—With one
exception,' he appended. 'In case you need anything
shifted, anything heavy, don't attempt it yourself, just
call Tim Westway. He's one of our regulars in the stacks,
and there's your house-phone—just whistle him up at any
time.'

'All right, I'll take care.' Her tone disparaged, none too
subtly, these excessive precautions. At that eminent
hunting-ground the Public Record Office, original correspondences of every famous name were put before the
researcher with regal largesse and with none of the fuss
that was being made over these muddled heaps from an
undistinguished country house. 'I'll take care,' she repeated slightingly. 'You and I and this Mr. Westway
when I need him, and no one else.'

'Thank you,' he returned. As the door closed behind
him she was thinking with dislike, *High and mighty you,
big frog, middling puddle.* Then she postponed recrim-
ination and let her eye range expertly in search of the
raggedest and presumably oldest deposits, as rough indications of a starting-point. Also, pulling on her overall,
she was glad to see the minute basin with soap and towel
laid on; after a session with such material one's hands
emerged black as from a coal-mine.

'I forgot to ask you something.' This was on her employer's second entrance. 'I usually go to lunch at one, so
would you mind arranging your own lunch earlier or

later? It's only,' he explained, 'so that both of us shan't be away at the same time.'

More precautions, she thought, *of all the hugger-mugger*, and replied decisively, 'I don't lunch, I'll just go out for a cup of tea about three. A steady five hours at this sort of thing is as much as I can take.'

'Of course. We've an electric kettle downstairs, Miss Carew'll show you—help yourself.'

'Thanks, but I prefer to go out.' With more effort than at first, she maintained her policy of unfriendliness. 'I need a little fresh air, after breathing solid dust.'

'As you like,' he nodded absently. 'Of course. Thank you.'

For some unknown reason his disappearance and the metallic snick of re-enclosure, instead of restoring her bastion of solitude against the outside world—the *safety* she hugged in these inviolate retreats of work—left behind a baffled and lonely moment, as if some defence she had trusted was to be trusted no longer. But the breach was so small that it closed over immediately, leaving the protective wall as strong as it ever had been. Or almost.

The soft knock at the door was startling because it recalled her from a trance of concentration, and because it was inexplicable; Durant would use his own key without knocking, so this could only be his secretary. . . . 'Miss Carew?' she called from where she sat on the floor in a waste of grimy documents.

Instead of an answer the soft knocking was repeated; impatiently she levered herself up, only then realizing the tightness of her neck and shoulderblades and the grittiness of her eyes into which some strands of hair had fallen and which she could not even push away, in view of the state of her hands. Holding these away from her like offensive foreign objects, she approached the door and called 'Yes?'

'It's me,' Myra announced ungrammatically from the other side of the barrier. Her voice was as soft and hurried as her knocking, and Alison had an impression that she was speaking right into the crack of the door.

'Yes, Myra, what is it?'

'Bally, for God's sake open up—don't keep me standing here with a cup of tea in my hands.'

'Oh.' Slightly surprised, she recalled her wits from other absorptions. 'Thank you, Myra, I don't want tea—not yet. But thank—'

'Of course you want tea,' the voice interrupted crossly. 'You've been at it since eleven or so, haven't you?'

Mention of the time drew her eyes automatically to her wrist; at once and by instinct her resistance stiffened before her consciousness could translate the source of this stiffening: *his lunch hour.*

'Oh, come on,' the voice adjured. 'Open up.'

'Myra, I'm sorry,' Alison strove, over her next inward query: *Where's Miss Carew? How did Myra get past her?* and upon her vision rose the probable answer. 'Mr. Durant said not—he said I wasn't to let anyone in.'

'Well of course, not just anyone—he didn't mean senior staff, you clot. Come on now, before this muck gets cold.'

'I can't let you in,' repeated the besieged. 'He told me not.'

'Not . . . .' echoed the voice, after a pause '—not *any-one?*'

'Not anyone. But thank you, I—'

A sound cut her off, a derisive hoot, and after the hoot,

'Well, I must say.' Then an offended laugh, too soprano. 'Never heard anything so damned silly in my whole life.'

'Sorry,' Alison repeated. 'Very—'

'Oh, stuff it,' said Myra vulgarly. 'All right, all right, Miss Hush-Hush.' The voice ceased; to the listener came the sense of a presence withdrawn, yet with no sound of departing footsteps. Nor, while she slowly returned and crouched once more in the litter, did this strike her as strange; it accorded with the pattern of the whole episode, and the pattern—she realized comprehensively —was stealth. No doubt that Myra had not only chosen the time of Durant's lunch hour, but also of Miss Carew's accustomed rendezvous with the electric kettle in the basement. All of it was furtive—the snatched opportunity, the muttering voice too close to the door, the soundless departure. And the cup of tea itself no real reason, only a pretext; with obscure uneasiness she felt Myra's desire —inexplicably urgent—to get into this room, along with her equally urgent wish not to be seen going to Durant's office, where almost certainly she had no business to be. Also, had she really not known that access to this room was forbidden, or was she pretending not to know . . . ?

She shook off these contending impressions, more puzzling than disturbing, and applied herself once more with unsparing minuteness. For all the predictable dulness of these domestic records in faded ink, hope illumined her with a fairly steady glow—the hope forever dashed and forever revived of unexpected treasure. Among the dingiest rubble of the past, among the most unpromising debris there might lurk some marvelous accident, some jewel as yet undiscovered. *You never knew,* faithfully she invoked the formula that spurred the weariest, most jaded researcher to fresh effort; *you never knew.*

The revolving afternoon brought her one more constraint she could well have dispensed with, but also an unexpected reward. The constraint was when she took her breather a little after three and happened to leave through the reading-room; Myra, only moderately busy at the counter, either did not see her or pretended not to see her. Feeling no guilt whatever, all the same she had the sense of trouble at relations adversely affected, and thought with angry discomfort, *I'd better use the staff entrance in future.*

The second, the reward, was no discovery of rare signatures or the like, but comforting all the same—a bonus called up from the stacks to shift a horrific pile of calf-bound ledgers so she might have a little more space. The Tim that her employer had mentioned she had visualized as the usual grimy troglodyte who would come shuffling up from the lower depths grudgingly, and whose grudging help she had better acknowledge with the occasional tip—strictly forbidden, but better that than constant obstructive surliness. She was familiar with this constant bugbear of libraries, the humbler staff invisible to the public and soon tiring of propelling book-trolleys to and fro with no prospect of gratuities or other extras; she had seen very august institutions constantly hiring and firing, for this donkey-work, elderly drifters just this side of derelict. Therefore her surprise and pleasure were understandably the greater when Tim materialized from the underworld with unorthodox promptness, an apparition diffusing—almost before he had said a word—the indefinable and all-conquering quality of *niceness*. He was eighteen or nineteen, she would guess, of average looks and sandy colouring; not actually tall but thin for his height, which made him look taller; his general appearance was dishevelled, the look of those who handle unwieldy dusty burdens all day. From this youthful being came a smile of uncalculating friendliness, and his, 'Yes, ma'am!' was enthusiastic invitation for orders, the more the better.

'You bet,' he attacked the ponderous tomes at her direction, and began hefting them. 'Golly, they're brutes all right,' he admitted. 'Valuable though, I expect?'

'I doubt it,' she smiled.

'Well, I'm glad you didn't tackle them yourself.' Quickly and efficiently he was stacking them against the wall. 'And mind you don't, just call me if there's anything to lug—just give me a shout.'

'Thank you very much,' she returned gratefully. 'I'll try not to shout too often, I expect you're busy.'

'Not all that busy,' he disclaimed light-heartedly. 'Call me any time, okey-doke?'

'Okey-doke,' she returned solemnly, and stood motionless a moment after he had gone. The first sight of him had reminded her, illogically, of Chris; illogically because there was no least resemblance between them, yet her heart had gone out to him. Still trammelled by this feeling, she tried in slow motion to resume work, then all at once was pierced with such longing for Chris—to see him, hear him for only one moment—that she had to sit perfectly still, fighting it, till it became too much for her. *Love is an ache*, she thought resignedly, getting up again and making for her handbag as for a last hope. From it she extracted a mounted snapshot and fortified herself with a long look before putting it back reluctantly and returning to the treadmill. Upon her face, bent once more to her drudgery, lingered and lingered a faint smile, till the dusty tide crept back and effaced it gradually. The smile was for her son, it belonged to him. But quite unknown to herself, Tim—who had sparked off that moment of awful yearning for Chris—shared in its softness and fondness a little, only a little.

IV

If her bedroom were made for lurking she would have lurked this evening, emerging only for dinner and going straight back. But her bedroom was not a retreat, only a sleeping-place; the low-wattage illumination, the absence of a really comfortable chair were deliberate, she had no doubt, to discourage undue use of current. This consideration pinned her where she stood, knowing her hesitation for the same thing that had pushed her out of the library a little before closing time—so that she need not walk home with Myra; all of it part of her wish, at least for the moment, to avoid Myra. A sudden resentment invaded her at having to spend herself in dodges and evasions instead of doing the natural thing, going downstairs for a few moments in the lounge before dinner. The utter isolation of her work made people painfully necessary to her at the day's end; not so much for talk as for the mere sight and sound of people about her. All at once her bedroom was unbearable, and its modest adequacy most unbearable of all. Yet her sudden plunge toward the door was halted, as her hand touched the knob, by a moment of new premonition. What if these lately-spun webs of constraint and embarrassment went on thickening and multiplying, day by day? Judging by developments so far, the prospect seemed likely. . . . .

'Hell,' she muttered, then thought, *Or am I making something out of nothing?*

With exaggerated force she pulled the door open and went downstairs.

In solitary and stately possession of the lounge was Mrs. Lees-Milburn. Majestic as a monolith she sat—naturally—in the most comfortable chair, so placed that no one else could get quite near enough to an adequate reading-light. Alison guessed that this good chair was hers by custom if not by right, and that it would take a bold spirit to contest her title. She noted likewise that the monolith was reading a newspaper, without glasses at that, and that her manner of raising her head at the newcomer's entrance was imperious but not actively hostile.

'Good evening,' Alison ventured.

'Good evening,' the harsh voice responded with un-expected civility, then to Alison's surprise the newspaper was laid down in favour of an obvious readiness to chat. 'And how do you like our village?'

'Lovely,' said Alison with truth. 'Lovely.'

'You are quite right,' said the ancient. 'And all of it is due to Lord Gurney, who will not let in the money-grubbers and tradespeople. I pray for his health,' she announced grandly, 'every night.'

'I see,' returned Alison, with a feeling that the Almighty would disregard the petitions of a Lees-Milburn at his peril.

'And do you intend,' the old woman pursued, 'to stop long among us?'

'Some weeks,' Alison conjectured. 'Some weeks at least, I expect.'

'Mr. Durant himself will have engaged you—?'

'Yes.'

'To sort out the Tollemache bequest, it would be?'

'Yes,' returned Alison, surprised at the knowledgeable allusion—then was diverted by the entrance of their landlady with the coffee-tray. This was a first opportunity to appraise her better than at their initial contact, when Mrs. Mowbray had shown her to her room and vanished, leaving behind her an impression of perpetual hurry. Now she could be seen as a taller-than-average woman of erect carriage, with the kind of figure once called 'handsome': her colouring, probably neutral in youth, betrayed her age less than if she had been decided blonde or brunette. Still possessing the distinction of her class— an effortless air of breeding—she was obviously carrying burdens she had not been brought up to carry, and carrying them moreover without complaint. This distinction of hers seemed as yet undimmed by drudgery, and along with her look of evident health and strength completed the picture of a stately ship kept afloat by the gallantry and resource of its commander.

'I hope you're comfortable, Miss Pendrell?' she asked, taking time to smile pleasantly at the newcomer.

'Very, thank you,' returned Alison, with a renewed sense of the woman's calm and imposing presence. 'Everything's lovely.'

'Caroline,' pronounced Mrs. Lees-Milburn, from her regal ensconcement, 'you work too hard.'

'Oh, one manages,' the other said off-handedly. 'If it were any other time of year, Miss Pendrell, you could sit in the garden.'

'Lovely garden,' said the armchair.

'Not any more, I fear.' Mrs. Mowbray was matter-of-fact. 'Nowadays one tries not to let it go to rack and ruin, but that's the most that can be said for it.'

'*Lovely* garden,' insisted the armchair loyally but absently, once more behind the newspaper.

Mrs. Mowbray said nothing, except that her glance went from Mrs. Lees-Milburn, hogging the light, and moved in silent apology to Alison. Her concealed smile admitted her helplessness, Alison's similar smile made light of the inconvenience, and the landlady thanked her guest with a look of charming warmth that lit her up amazingly, and quite differently from her professional smile. Her departure left Alison curiously envious— envious of such unforced moral stateliness, such natural, imperturbable serenity. From this awareness she was jerked in short order; the old woman only waited for the door to close before resuming, 'So you have been engaged by Mr. Durant. He is of very old and excellent family from hereabouts, and so was Miss Tollemache. So am I,' she interpolated. 'So is Mrs. Mowbray. And all of us poor now—Miss Tollemache died without a bean.' Her tone was factual and indifferent. 'But Tom Durant is very well paid, I expect— Ah, Juno!' She broke off to acclaim the dog, which had shouldered in like a baby elephant; the door must have been slightly off the latch. 'Was she the *lovely* girl then? Was she the *clever* girl?—The door if you would, Miss Pendrell, the draught—' Her peremptory tone, with its assumption of obedience, had raised Alison hypnotically from her chair when the door opened again.

The effect of this addition to their party was curious. At sight of Myra the old woman, without moving an inch, contrived to suggest a retreat to distant and inaccessible altitudes. Simultaneously she continued fondling the dog and murmuring endearments, a running accompaniment to any conversation essayed against it.

'D'you feel like a little walk before dinner, Bally?'
Myra's voice was too casual, her ignoring of Mrs. Lees-
Milburn too pointed; in the technique of silent insult she
could not begin to compete with the older product.

'Oh thank you, Myra, no,' Alison refused at once, her
instinct several jumps ahead of thought.

'Come on, you lazy thing.' Myra's playful tone was
patently synthetic. 'Get the cobwebs out of your brain.'

'No thanks—it's beastly outside.'

'But just a *tiny* walk—?'

'I wouldn't go out again,' Alison returned with conviction, 'for anything.'

A pause followed, full of her awareness of Myra's
strenuous desire for private conversation, and her equally
strenuous determination to avoid it. Here was another
strand of the trammelling web she had foreseen, the
vista of laborious feints and evasions. Yet somehow,
while holding off Myra, she must contrive to be friendly;
contrive not to give more offence, on top of what she had
already given. . . . .

'Before we were interrupted, Miss Pendrell,' Mrs. Lees-
Milburn put in with unnatural suavity, breaking off her
communion with the dog, 'I would have guessed, at haz-
ard, that your family background was not commercial?'

'No.' Mere unreadiness jolted Alison into vital statistics.
'My father was a clergyman in Oxfordshire, and a terribly
unsuccessful farmer.'

'Gentry,' murmured the inquirer. 'One can always tell.'
With similar abruptness she returned to Juno; during a
microscopic pause Myra's eyes slid toward the old
woman, once, and slid back. While Alison held her breath
in expectation of developments—reprisal must surely

follow on provocation so baldly offered—the dinner-gong began spreading its edgeless clamour through the house.

Even en route to table she scented trouble ahead; moreover, while seating herself—as if this act possessed some mysterious power of clarification—two undeveloped facets of her unease hardened and became sharp and distinct. One was her augmented sense of Myra's irritation at being balked of their private conference, and the conviction that she would take it out, at the first opportunity, on a target too-easily guessed. The other was a memory from college days that Myra, for all her high spirits and tumultuous generosities, was a creature of dark moods and a very poor forgiver. Then, too forcibly, she attempted to discount her premonition. Granted that Myra's desire for revenge would inevitably be aimed at Mrs. Lees-Milburn, how did a woman so young pick, with any decency, a quarrel with a woman so old?

Her momentary preoccupation with these matters delayed her recognition of something else—an absentee at table—and for another brief interval was fully occupied with regret.

'Mr. Durant dines this evening with Lady Russell,' Mrs. Lees-Milburn announced with mysterious satisfaction, during an initial deployment of soup-spoons. 'She told me so.'

A slight but audible sniff was easily attributable to Myra, though Alison happened not to be looking her way at the moment.

'You will be interested to know, Miss Pendrell—' the old woman's extra blandness denoted how pleasurably she was invigorated by the sniff '—that Mr. Durant is enabled to do the library an amazing deal of good, merely

in having access to our county families. As,' she added
pointedly, 'as an equal.'

'County families,' Myra observed dreamily, to no one
in particular. 'I thought all that'd gone out with the dodo.'

'To many it might appear so,' remarked Mrs. Lees-
Milburn serenely—also not to Myra but to the circum-
ambient air. 'To persons outside our class, who are as
little qualified to judge as, say, a Pakistani just smuggled
in. Miss Pendrell—'

Alison, unfairly swept into the arena, experienced a
moment of unqualified consternation.

'—would you not agree that a civilization nearly a
thousand years old,' the mischief-maker pursued inexorably, 'cannot be demolished all that quickly by a horde
of Welfare parasites and their vulgar political messiahs?
I grant you,' she conceded royally, 'that they are doing
their best, and have made great inroads upon our England, and will in time destroy it. But not yet,' she
perorated. 'Not quite yet.'

Relief dawned in Alison, also realization. Welcome relief that there was no need to answer questions which
were not questions, only a series of thrusts at Myra; and
realization, not welcome, that Mrs. Lees-Milburn was
using her as a sounding-board off which she could bounce
other verbal projectiles, always to the same address. Resentment at this last awareness somehow did not obscure
still another awareness—of the constriction in Myra's
face, and of how it was becoming progressively more
spiteful.

'As I was saying,' the old woman proceeded majesti-
cally, 'Mr. Durant has influenced people to bequeath to
the library valuable family documents, which for a
stranger they would not have done. I myself,' she
preened, 'am leaving my dear mother's papers and

correspondence to the Champernowne. A splendid acquisition for them—most important.'

'Important?' Myra put in gently, almost dreamily. 'How important?'

Electric foreboding stabbed through Alison and tingled in her scalp. Myra had made the first move in her campaign of denigrating the quality of the letters, in hopes to madden her opponent into displaying them. With excitement, apprehension and undeniable curiosity she awaited the outcome of what promised to be mortal combat.

'Just how well did this Mrs. Wavenell know Browning?' Myra pursued into a paralyzed silence. 'The real Browning circle were all in Italy, during Elizabeth's lifetime. Mrs. Wavenell wasn't one of that lot—that much I'll tell you right now.'

'My dear mother,' said Mrs. Lees-Milburn, frigid and yet imperfectly-recovered, 'was his—his—'

Both women continued speaking not to, but at each other, each one addressing the air over the other's head.

'Her name hardly appears—' Myra, interrupting in a drawl, flourished a new red rag '—in any biography of Browning that I ever saw. And only in passing mention —never prominently.'

'B-Browning—' furious, the old woman fought Myra's literacy with family tradition '—was my mother's intimate f-friend.'

'Oh, I don't doubt she *knew* him.' Myra's tone was a masterpiece of disparagement. 'Like a thousand other society women who chased him because he was famous, and who couldn't have got through one of his longer poems to save their lives.'

'His—his letters,' sputtered the ancient. 'His letters to my m-mother—'

'What sort of letters?' Myra, springing the mine, smiled a small deadly smile. 'He was a crashing old snob in his later life, always popping off little notes to duchesses about lunch-parties, stuff like that. If that's the sort of stuff he wrote to Mrs. Wavenell, it's worth almost nothing. Even the autographs aren't valuable—he left too many of them.'

The table by now was unnaturally silent; hands and jaws continued the automatic movements of feeding, while all eyes swivelled hypnotically between the combatants.

'A fruitless discussion, quite fruitless,' the old woman essayed. 'With one who has enjoyed no access to these documents.—Not,' she loosed an unexpected shaft '—not for lack of trying.'

The sudden hot crimson of Myra's face, the baleful whites of her eyes, acknowledged not only the hit, but the enemy's recovery of ground. Yet rallying almost at once—

'There's something a tiny bit odd,' she cooed as if in soliloquy, 'about refusing to submit even a few of such letters to expert examination. Of course if they prove that Mrs. Wavenell was only another minor literary hostess, and that Browning knew her only superficially, I'd quite understand the refusal—'

'Come, come, Myra.'

Alison's easy uncombative tone belied her own surprise at thrusting between the antagonists, but something in the old woman's face—its anger and desperately-beleaguered look—had alarmed her. 'Browning loved his late success and especially loved attentions from women, he was happy and warm and frank about it. I don't doubt in the least he was on good terms with Mrs. Wavenell and fond of her.'

'He was fond,' gibed Myra, 'of every Tom, Dick and Harry.'

'Yes, he was a natural lover of people,' Alison agreed blandly. 'What's wrong with that?'

'Just as others,' chipped in Mrs. Lees-Milburn, sensationally revived by support, 'are natural haters. Especially,' she subjoined, 'of superiority—*any* kind.'

The lounge and its exclusive possession by the old woman and herself—Alison realized by now, with a sinking heart—was a matter of daily occurrence. Myra and the Major made short work of their coffee and disappeared, Durant never seemed to be in for dinner, Mr. Marcus never presumed—which inevitably reduced the population to two. How gladly Alison would have reduced it by a further fifty percent only she herself knew, but one thing drove her to make a stand. She loved her after-dinner coffee; to linger over it was one of her scanty pleasures, to sit luxurious and lazy, thinking of nothing and absorbing a first and a second cup drop by drop. To find herself caught between the alternatives of giving up this nirvana or of supporting the whole weight of Mrs. Lees-Milburn's presence, raised all her hackles of resistance. It was too much, being pushed here and there by pressures that were none of her making and of which she had known nothing a week ago; it would become intolerable if she let it. . . . She would not let it; beneath her quiet exterior were resistance and resolution, yet under them again a weariness of being forced to decision. . . .

Meanwhile in this present coffee-interlude, and faced with the usual company, with grim inward amusement she was diagnosing accurately her companion's uncharacteristic silence. This pent-up seething, a hangover of the dinner altercation, could not be contained for long; the old woman must soon blow off steam, she had nothing to do but wait. . . .

'Will you believe, Miss Pendrell—' the dowager's voice was more abrupt, harsh and grating than usual '—that that person, that MacKinnon woman, once suggested to me that I sell some or all of my mother's correspondence? *sell* them?'

'Did she?' Alison's neutral query was superimposed on a background of surprise; Myra, in speaking of the letters, had certainly not mentioned any such attempt on her part.

'She did indeed!' affirmed Mrs. Lees-Milburn. 'And barely knowing me at that, being barely on terms of acquaintance, can you imagine? The effrontery!'

Alison's vague murmur was drowned beneath the onrush of indignation, contempt, and other emotional secretion.

'I couldn't believe my ears,' she rasped. 'Such presumption. All the same I tried not to be too unkind at first go-off, you know, I was hardly more than distant. But d'you suppose that made any impression on her? Not in the least! She came worming back with more of the same, so persistent it passes belief. Didn't even realize what a gross liberty she was taking. Too thick-skinned— too common.'

'I shouldn't call her common,' Alison demurred, but out of an eroded conviction. The truth was—she found all at once—that her impaired relations with Myra had subtly impaired her loyalty; if not precisely willing to go on listening, she was not unwilling. In addition, there was Myra's censored account of the story—of which she was inclined to believe the present version; also there was Myra's determined attempt to get into the forbidden room and her resentment at being thwarted, a resentment somehow out of proportion. . . .

'I put her in her place, I promise you,' said Mrs. Lees-Milburn, bridling at even the suggestion of argument. 'I never liked her from the first, I know the type too well. A lower housemaid, that's the most she could aspire to in any establishment *I've* ever known.'

'No,' Alison contravened, with firm ground under her feet. 'She had a scholarship at Somerville—she was considered brilliant, definitely.'

'Gorbals,' sneered the ancient. 'Or I shouldn't wonder.'

'All the more credit to her,' Alison averred stoutly, 'that she's pulled herself out of it by her own efforts.'

'These slum-types that manage to get themselves over-educated,' said Mrs. Lees-Milburn with fastidious, implacable disdain, 'on scholarships provided by people of our class, not theirs—all that can't change them from what they really are. It's *in* them, and you can't educate it out. Your Miss MacKinnon with her degrees and diplomas, all that nonsense—the moment I saw her I'd just one word for her, straightaway.' The old woman gathered herself and put her whole soul into a final effort. '*Low*. Low, insolent, thrusting little vulgarian.'

A lovely beginning for the weekend, she reflected in her room; tides of hostility already running high on Friday evening, with two more days in which to run higher. Her own position in all this seemed deplorably clear. Myra's first grudge over the locked door would now be aggravated by her championship of the enemy force at dinner. Through this championship she had probably incurred the old woman's favour, which would rub Myra still more the wrong way. That she wanted no part of this favour—that she repudiated her role as a dumping-

THE FOURTH MAN ON THE ROPE 63

ground of antagonisms—would do her no service whatever; she had been elected as confidante by both parties,
without her consent.

Therefore the immediate problem (exclusive of sub-
sidiary ones) was how to get through the weekend without involving herself still further. The only answer, total
avoidance of both combatants, was as wishful as im-
practicable. Maddening to find herself trapped in other
people's squabbles, practically from the very outset. . . .

In the end she found the impasse compelling her to
evasive measures, and that evasion was foreign to her
nature hardly made it more soothing. She threw a few
things into her smallest case, to have it ready against the
morning. Then she went to bed; scuttling in her mind
from one expedient to another had exhausted her. Men-
tally she set the reliable alarm-clock that would rouse her
early enough to miss breakfast, to ring for a taxi, and to
be on an early train for London.

Through the wet murk beginning to descend so soon
as four o'clock, the lights of Mowbray's seemed, to the
returning wanderer, not unwelcoming. On the way from
Folkestone she had had time to estimate that although
her flight had cost her nothing but her cheap return
and two taxi fares, the gain from it was invisible and the
loss perceptible. Twenty-six hours alone in an empty flat
had given her what she wanted, a chance to think without being belaboured. Her thinking had been to so little
effect—so disconnected and inconclusive—that by one-
thirty on Sunday she was en route again for Charing
Cross. One thing alone, out of all the sterile weekend,
was clear to her as she climbed the guest-house steps.
Out of mere stupid unreadiness and cowardice she had

been pushed into running away once: she would not run away again.

She let herself in and was cheered by the sight of Mrs. Mowbray in the hall, her serene and handsome presence immeasurably soothing; the benign and impregnable rock that upheld, in this house, the atmosphere of home. . . .

'Mrs. Mowbray,' Alison besought. 'I know I haven't ordered tea in advance, but would it be too much trouble to ask for a cuppa, and—and anything else that's going?'

'Naturally you shall have a cuppa,' smiled the other. 'A bit tired, are you? By the time you've taken your things upstairs, I'll have it ready for you in the lounge.'

She disappeared before Alison could voice a hesitant request; how dearly she would have loved to carry the tray upstairs and have it in solitude before her own gas-fire . . . more running away, she thought, the very thing she had sworn against, and stiffened inwardly. A few minutes later, descending again, she opened the lounge door firmly upon the accustomed spectacle. Mrs. Lees-Milburn looked up from behind her outspread newspaper, nodded, and returned to her reading without a word; Alison already knew that this session with the public news-prints was a sacred ritual, not to be profaned by any interruption, on any account.

The pot of tea was there, flanked by a plate of bread-and-butter and cake; the fresh hot liquid revived her so magically that her inability to touch the food surprised her. At once she realized that it was the unresolved anxieties generated by Myra that had taken away her usually healthy appetite; something else to check up to Myra's account. . . .

While she sat with this new thought, angrily burning

her lips and throat in spite of the smallest of swallows, she became aware that Mrs. Lees-Milburn, still totally absorbed in the newspaper to all outward appearance, by some occult means was shooting small forked lightnings of awareness in her general direction and managing to do this, moreover, without a single direct glance. Quickly realizing her untouched plate as the target about which these lightnings flickered, and noting now that the old woman's tea consisted of the pot and cup lonely and ungarnished, Alison said with hesitation, 'Mrs. Lees-Milburn, I wonder if I might offer you these biscuits?'

'Why—' With well-bred and plausible surprise, the ancient emerged from behind her rampart. 'Why, how very nice of you. But aren't you having any yourself?'

'Not any, thanks.'

'You're sure?'

'Quite.' Alison cut short the charade of courtesies by rising and setting the plate firmly alongside the other. Mrs. Lees-Milburn's regal nod of acceptance made it clear, by some tenuous magic, that she was conferring a benefit rather than accepting a kindness. At once she fell upon the small gift and was champing away with undisguised relish as Alison returned to her seat and her cogitations which became—all at once and once for all— ironclad. From now on, where Myra was concerned, she would not skulk and she would not propitiate. Whatever resentments Myra chose to display—and they were inevitable—she would meet with unshakable politeness; not with indifference, for that was alienating, but with an amiability imperturbable, and above all not nervous. . . .

At this point in her review of policy the lounge door opened but closed again—too quickly to see who it was, but she had not needed to see. Who but one person would do such a thing, who else would stoop to a ploy so furtive. . . .

She excused herself from dinner on the count of tiredness. She knew it was not tiredness but nervous indigestion; it had taken only that quick opening and shutting of the door to plow her up again, just when she had calmed herself with judicious and admirable resolutions. She could abjure cowardice but not the symptoms of cowardice, and with perfect awareness of her state lay on nettles of perfect self-contempt. Having run away once and sworn against such shabby performance, she could do no better—by missing dinner—than run away again.

V

Myra walked with her to the library on Monday morning.

'Wherever did you get to,' she asked at once, 'over the weekend?'

'Some things I had to see to in London.' Alison's tone, her glance fixed straight ahead, were irreproachably pleasant, also impervious enough to repulse even Myra from the smiling barrier. During a silence in which they needed all their breath—today's wind was aftermath of a storm that had lashed the coast violently all day Sunday —she felt without seeing Myra's occasional sidewise glance, her air of canvassing another avenue of approach; while grateful for the postponement so kindly engineered by nature, she recognized that it would run out with the first lull of wind, and in fact did so run out.

'You were certainly chatting up that horrid little man at breakfast.' Myra struck from a totally-unexpected quarter. 'That Marcus.'

'I said good morning, and he said good morning,' Alison returned. 'He said it was a little better day than yesterday, and I said yes, it was—if you call that chatting him up.'

'Those were *your* biscuits that old scavenger was gobbling in the lounge,' the other accused. 'She can't afford the full tea.'

Between the opening and shutting of the door, thought Alison, she had managed to see that.

'She can't afford the pot either.' Myra, discarding show-gambits, went full force for the real objective. 'I'll bet Caroline Mowbray lets her have it for what they were paying before World War I.'

'She might as well have had the biscuits,' shrugged Alison. 'I didn't want them.'

'She'd eat findings out of a dust-bin, that one would,' said Myra, 'if she could do it without being seen.'

'By the way.' Alison, wearied with one-way vitupera-tion, mounted an attack of her own. 'By what she said during that row of yours at dinner, it sounds as though you'd made much more effort to see her letters than you've told me—?'

'Well yes, I did.' Myra answered with minimum hesi-tation, and hardly at all abashed. 'You know how people in our line're in touch with dealers—in manuscripts and autographs etcetera. Well, they're all desperate for ma-terial, you know that. So I didn't see how it would do any harm if I could get a look at them, or get her to . . . . show just a few to some expert, someone really first-class? Where was the harm in that?'

'No harm,' Alison murmured neutrally. 'No harm at all.'

'I didn't mention it to you, I expect, because there was nothing to mention—just a trial balloon that never went up. But of course you know,' Myra pursued, 'that if one puts a dealer in the way of material, it's always worth a commission—which God knows I can always use. To say nothing,' she appended virulently, 'of how *she* could use a good price for them and pay her way a bit more, in-stead of scrounging on that angel Caroline Mowbray. God, could she use it!'

'But she didn't take kindly—' Alison's question, blatantly superfluous, came from a curiosity as blatantly roused '—to the idea?'

'Take kindly? You heard her, didn't you? She's hated my guts ever since. I've desecrated the shrine—committed grade-A blasphemy.—And why,' Myra demanded, coming to the point at last, 'did you take her part the other evening, against me? She's overbearing enough as it is, offensive old bully.'

'Old,' Alison stressed, but with conciliation. 'You were upsetting her, and she's old.'

'Old!' Myra began scornfully, then in the very act of rebuttal went unnaturally still, her combativeness arrested—or at least postponed—by some other caprice of her swooping, veering thoughts.

'Did Durant actually tell you that no one was to be let in where you're working?' she said finally, yet with a curious absent effect of something else on her mind. 'Actually, *no* one?'

'No one at all,' Alison apologized.

'Well, I call it an insult to staff. As if he didn't trust us.' But again some restraint in her made the words unaggressive, almost perfunctory; while her companion fumbled with these gaps of contradiction Myra, harking back, had said, 'So you're Lees-Milburn's little pet.' Still prolific in inconsistencies, her tone was less jeering than reflective, and less reflective than calculating.

'Sooner you than me,' she gibed in the next moment, with another of her lightning changes of subject and mood.

As they entered the library Alison had time for a sudden irrelevant thought: that only Durant's absence the other night had emboldened Myra to attack the old woman as she had done; she would never have dared to

do it in his presence. . . . All at once she was swept by
gratitude for her workroom with its welcoming peace
and silence; her sanctuary that healed her of all these
clashes and broils with its antidote of things long past,
its embalmed and cloistral calm.

The calm proved neither so embalmed nor so invincible as she had rashly assumed; the missile that ruptured
it was flung without warning while she was teasing apart
some papers matted into a clump by mould and damp.
Astounded she raised her head, gaping with sheer unbelief. Of all unlikely sounds in this scholarly atmosphere
this was the most unlikely, yet undeniable—a woman's
voice, raised on the note of strident quarrelsomeness. The
irruption made her realize that she had been aware of
voices next door for some time, with unhearing awareness, till this one shot up to the highest reach of invective.

'You selfish beast!' it yelled. 'God, you contemptible
. . . you corpse, that's all you are! *dead,* dead as all that
rotten stupid muck you're always dredging up from
some rotten old house. Papers, *Christ—*!'

On the final word the voice broke with sheer rage;
simultaneously the flaw in her inviolacy became evident
—the door between herself and Durant, a massive mahogany door superbly fitted yet shrunken enough by
passing centuries to let in sound, much more sound than
she wanted to hear . . . in panic she rose and scrambled
foolishly to the farthest limits of the room, and relent-
lessly the voice pursued her.

'Will you give me the house?' it panted on a rising note.
'Will you give me it? will you?'

'It's not mine to give.' Durant's tone, quenched by a
chronic weariness, was audible if only just. 'It's not my
house, it's my father's.'

'So what? he'll give it to you if you ask for it.—Or don't ask for the house.' Suddenly the voice was infused with new and hopeful briskness. 'Ask him for a power of attorney, then you can give the house to me.'

A laugh, grim and brief, preceded the answer. 'Give you the house? behind his back?'

'Why ever not? what difference can it make to him? He'll never come out of that nursing-home alive.—Tom, see here.' The voice, dropping lower, carried by weight of menace if no longer by volume. 'All along you've made difficulties, you've done everything to spoil things for me—'

'I've told you time and again.' Durant interrupted on a raised note of opposition. 'You can have your divorce, I shan't interfere.'

'Generous of you, dear, but the divorce isn't enough. Basil thinks I've got money—'

'You've had every spare penny of mine.'

'Bah, those few miserable thousands! And they're running out, I've *told* you I'm feeling the pinch. But that big barrack standing empty in that enormous garden, and builders paying the earth for anything thereabout, simply the earth!—Tom, just . . . . just feel him out on the subject. *Please—!*'

'Esmé—'

Esmé; how very Michael Arlen, thought Alison, stabbed by malice, then surprised by the sharpness of the stab.

'—I shan't ask my father anything.' His voice was now raised above his wife's. 'I won't hound a dying man, and make up your mind to that.'

'Dying! he's been dying forever. He can go on dying another few centuries, while Basil loses interest in me. A quick divorce and some money and we'll marry, yes,

but if things drag on and on and he finds out that all
I've got is that pittance—'

An interjection, inaudible.

'—well, what if he is? Who *is* disinterested? Men are
all the same—rotten. He wants to be sure of some money
and I don't blame him, I like money myself. And Basil's
fun! He's fun to be with, he's got something on his mind
beside wormy old books—*Tom.*'

Into that *Tom* had come a new note, ominous.

'Now once and for all, look.' Her every syllable drilled
through the door with its forced calm. 'I'm being generous. I'm letting you divorce me for adultery, instead of
the other way around. But I warn you: if I lose Basil because your father keeps hanging on, no divorce, not ever.
I'll be about your neck as long as I live, and don't think
I'll make it easy for you. I'll follow you about, I'll make
such stinking rows in public places it'll be impossible for
those Governors of yours to keep you here—'

Strange: of all the tirade it was that phrase, *instead of
the other way around,* that enclosed her in a total deafness. Oblivious of all but its implication she missed a number of words, then woke to the dialogue's changed
nature.

'—I don't want to do it the hard way,' Mrs. Durant
was protesting on a note of odious blandishment. 'Why
drive me into it? If I had the house, we'd all be happy.
I'd marry Basil and be out of your hair, and *you* . . .'

From wheedling the voice had become—all at once—
sly.

'—you could marry that woman you've got. Oh, you've
been clever about keeping her hidden, but I know about
her, all right. You could marry her,' she repeated. 'She's
probably panting for marriage, the dirty slut.'

Pause.

'All you have to do—' on an accent of intense reason-
ableness '—is ask your father for the house or a power of
attorney. He'll give you anything, you know he will. Ask
him, Tom—all you've to do is ask him.'

His reply, inaudible, touched off an eruption that left
no doubt of its nature.

'All right!' she shrieked. 'All right, damn you, damn you
to hell—spoil my life and what for, an old bag of bones!
Why someone hasn't put him out of his misery long ago,
your father—all right, all right, but you'll wish you'd done
differently, you miserable, rotten, stupid . . . damn you
to hell, you'll be sorry—!'

The outer door shattered cataclysmically on the heels
of the final screech.

A silence followed, unnatural; moving slowly from her
futile retreat, she felt this silence clairvoyantly as spreading from his office and imposing itself upon every room
off the staff corridor. She had heard the onslaught with
horrid distinctness through the misfortune of special
propinquity, but the other offices—the Assistant Librarian, secretary and others—must have heard enough; the
shindy at its height might even have carried as far as the
public reading-room. . . . Then a curious knowledge
took her, a certainty that Thomas Durant's staff conspired
to hide his shame; that on every hand there would be a
strenuous ignorance of what had passed. Then and
there she entered into the conspiracy with all her heart,
on the evil chance of its ever being necessary. . . .

Again she listened; again, nothing but silence. All at
once she found herself too unsettled to work, and with a
violent need to get out and walk off tension and a slight
headache. Her watch said half-past one. Usually he went
out at one, and today he might have left immediately
after his ruinous visitor. But she had to make sure; it was

simply not possible to walk out through his room if he were still there. . . .

Holding her breath she turned the key with infinite caution, and by its silent working of ancient craftsmanship was able to open the door a hair's-breadth and peer out—at the back of his head and shoulders. He was sitting perfectly still at his desk, and even her glimpse of this stillness disquieted her. She closed the door again with the same noiseless stealth, and resigned herself to restless waiting—restless with her own unrest and not at all with hunger. After more anxious listening without the least informative sound next door, she invented a pretext and rang Tim in the basement. Admitting him, and carefully not looking out, she asked, 'Does it seem to disturb Mr. Durant, when you come through his office?'

'He's not there,' he reassured. 'Yes, ma'am, what wants doing?'

As soon as he left she shot out, holding her breath against the possibility of meeting whom she most wanted to avoid, but gaining the street unscathed. Already she felt better, then realized that Tim was the restorative; after that scalding eruption of greed what a relief this boy with his untainted, uncalculating blitheness. . . .

Her soft incipient smile died abruptly with the thought of Durant, humiliated and scarified by scenes like the one she had heard. Myra was quite right; one of them one day would explode into raw scandal, and he would be asked (however regretfully) to resign his position. *Why doesn't someone murder her?* she wondered fervently, and at once doused her fervour with cold water of remembrance: *I'm letting you divorce me for adultery, instead of the other way around . . . you've been clever about keeping her hidden but I know, all right.* . . . .

'Be calm, Miss Galahad,' she told herself ironically.

'He's got someone, he's all right.' Pleased to find how much this reminder buttressed her withdrawal, she pursued silently, *It's his affair, he'll straighten it out himself and he's quite up to it too. Don't be zealous,* she adjured herself cruelly. *All he needs in his life is more female championship. A week ago you'd never so much as set eyes on him.*

With this resolute attainment of indifference—comforting as all definite attitude is comforting—all the same she indulged in a passing lament, a faint irrepressible valediction: *Why is it that a man like that, the sort one never sees or almost never, is never ever free? Here's this one up to his neck in a rotten marriage, and before he's even clear of it, someone's already grabbed him—*

A violent check and self-awareness broke upon her, through the unlikely medium of her own two feet. She stopped dead and stared down at them in their walking shoes, substantial and well-polished—hallmark, as Myra had said, of dull respectable drudgery. *Well, and supposing he were free,* she mocked herself, *why should he look at you, a dowdy, clumsy, thick . . .*

More damagingly still, far more damagingly, she perceived such alien longings for what they were: a threat to her whole way of life, sexless, industrious and thrifty; a threat to her triumphant elimination of everything not for Chris. This was her amends to Chris for giving him a useless father; her way of making sure he would lack for nothing because she, with pulpy romantic bad judgment, had surrendered to a mass of vicious qualities beneath a beautiful male exterior. Now, with this momentary betrayal of Chris—the treachery of wanting something for herself—her daily life gave way beneath her feet and let her drop sickeningly; like the time when, working on the college show, she had confidently set foot on what she took to be a catwalk and dropped twelve feet to the stage below. The shock and jar then were hardly less than the shock and jar she felt now; the feeling of displacement, of being suddenly adrift. . . .

She put it aside and faced the imminent problem. She was bound to come face to face with Durant in a short time, and wondered how the two of them would carry it off. With concealed embarrassment? a mutual pretence that none of it had happened? True, he could not tell precisely how much she had heard, but must know it was more than enough. Awkward that he should be forced—before a newcomer on his staff—into a pose either false or constraining, poor unlucky man. . . .

Being sorry for him strengthened her still more; in pity there was always ascendancy. Entering the library with a brisk step, her face had cleared of concern and even become faintly complacent as she cast herself in the role of perfect collaborator. He had to save face by pretending, and she would help him to the limit. Let him indicate the pattern, and with tactful understanding—perfect and consummate tact—she would follow.

He was sitting at his desk, and raised his head as she walked in. As expected, yet something—some intangible reason—made her falter. Before her discomfort could betray her further he had said, 'I hope that row in here didn't disturb you unduly.'

'Why . . .' Between floundering, and the effort of seeming not to flounder, she disclaimed weakly, 'Not— not much, not—'

'I'd no warning of it myself, or I should have warned you,' he pursued. 'Well, not to bore you, there've been some preliminary bouts, but not anything quite like this. It's merely unfortunate that your arrival here coincides with a crisis in my wife's affairs, probably a quite serious crisis for her. And as you've just heard, she's inclined to meet crises with violence.'

She was silent, still unsettled by his failure to beat about the bush.

'There's no use pretending these things haven't happened, when they have happened,' he pursued with the same detachment. 'Moreover, and more practically, I can't guarantee to prevent them. I can't refuse my wife access, and alternatively I can't have her removed as a disturbance. But I owe you an abject apology—you must have been considerably shocked.'

'Not shocked,' she protested falsely. 'A bit startled perhaps.'

'So all I can do at the moment,' he waived her politeness, 'is beg you to put up with the situation—take it in your stride. That is,' he qualified, 'if I'm not asking too much.'

'No,' she returned, pleased to match his impersonality with an impersonality nearly as accomplished. He had put an impossible situation on the most possible and sensible basis. Also it was salutary to know—in case her admiration for him revived inconveniently—that she had a formula always guaranteed to quench it: *I'm letting you divorce me for adultery, instead of the other way around.*

'Well?' Myra demanded, indecently agog. 'I wasn't exaggerating, was I?'

Whatever one's stratagems of avoidance, thought Alison, Myra was bound to nail you in the end; the thought took precedence in her somewhat fumbling search for an answer.

'Now that you've had one of her ragmatags under your

very nose . . .' she was pressing on '. . . why, I even thought I heard something in the reading-room. I was listening for it, you bet—soon as I'd seen her go in. Lucky you, right at the horse's mouth!' Again her glance skewered, sharpened with greed and envy. 'Bally, what happened? exactly what is it she's playing him up for, poor devil?'

'I don't know,' Alison countered. Her disclaimer—too prompt for tact, too unyielding for apology—was toughened furthermore by involuntary distaste. Its impact must have pierced a skin thicker than that of Myra, who met its flat rebuff with flat silence, before commenting, 'That's likely,' and with barely a pause tightened her nuance of enquiry to demand. 'What do you mean, you don't know?'

'I mean I don't know.' Imbecile response, a litany that could go on forever. 'I wasn't listening and I didn't want to listen.'

'But how could you help—why, the woman was letting off like a siren. You heard every word of it, you didn't need to listen.'

'Well, I didn't.' With heartening unconcern she brushed off Myra's insistence, then (spineless as usual, she thought) offered a sop. 'You couldn't hear it actually, except when she blew up now and again. Anyway, I'd have been ashamed to listen.'

The silence this time was noticeably prolonged; on its heels Myra said, 'I get it.' Her waspishness was remarkable. 'The penny's dropped at last. You've joined the elite, have you? the inner circle?'

'What inner circle?'

'The Durant Female Protective League.' The capital letters were audible. 'The so-discreet secretary, the so-discreet assistant, and now the so-discreet hired help. My apologies, I'm sure,' she minced venomously. 'Asking you to break your oath. I'll know better next time.' She bent upon her companion a look perfectly blank of expression, yet more disquieting in its blankness than the most flaming resentment.

It was a pattern, this after-dinner captivity; a pattern that she had allowed first to coagulate, then to harden about her, and from which—short of walking out brutally —she could see no present escape. Failing the nerve for brutality she seemed doomed to sit as she sat now, torpidly watching Mrs. Lees-Milburn as she fished from her lumpy old handbag, and peeled unconcernedly, tablets of sugar—pilfered from different tea-rooms, to judge by the variety of their wrappings. 'I steal sugar for horses,' she had confessed once, archly. It seemed however that she divided this philanthropy between her equine friends and her own coffee-cup; absorbed contentedly, and without a shade of embarrassment, in supplementing her genteel spoonful from the official bowl. The small mystery was where she obtained her plunder, since even the cheapest restaurants were beyond her. Friends must take her out once in a while, Alison decided sleepily, it was the only answer. . . .

'I understand,' the raucous old voice cut through her half-doze, 'that Esmé Durant was seen in the village this morning.'

Alison blinked, looked up, and found herself spiked on a gaze of bright malicious curiosity.

'Esmé,' the old woman pursued. 'What a name! And if she's about, there's bound to be trouble.'

'Oh?' Alison murmured vacantly, and in haste gathered her wits about her.

'I was only hoping,' the ancient pursued, 'that she

hadn't made some beastly row in Tom's office.' Her
glance, this time, bypassed curiosity for open invitation.
'She's quite capable of it, in fact I believe she's been
known to do something of the sort, before now . . . ?'

'Has she?' To the flagrant cue she opposed a blindness
and deafness as flagrant. 'I'm a newcomer here, you
know.'

'But in the library itself,' the old woman fished tena-
ciously, 'one couldn't help hearing—?'

'Perhaps not.' Plainly Mrs. Lees-Milburn had got wind,
however vaguely, of today's episode. 'Provided one happened to be nearby when the trouble started.'

'I see.' The old woman's baffled look and tone con-
veyed, with pyrotechnic skill, other things as well; a mocking scepticism yet a mocking approval, grim, of such
invincible discretion. 'You've not seen her then, Esmé Durant?'

'No.'

'I expect you'll have that pleasure one day,' the other
assured her. 'I've often wondered she hasn't got herself
strangled before now, what with the sort of people she
takes up with.'

She dropped the matter conclusively and entered into
a rapt communion with her coffee-cup, at whose bottom
she must have built up by now a half-inch sludge of illicit
sugar. While she sat spooning up semi-solid beads of amber and sipping them slowly in a voluptuous trance of
pleasure, her companion lapsed into meditation. Two at-
tacks on her reticence so far, concerning Esmé Durant;
the old woman had taken her defeat well, and Myra had
taken it badly. Add this new grudge to the flourishing
list Myra already had against her, and there could be
little doubt—considering Myra's temperament—that some
manifestation against her must result. Not at once, per-

haps not even soon; in its nature unpredictable, but predictably of glass-house nurture—ripeness of growth, revealed in ripeness of time.

'Alison,' said Myra, 'I'd like to talk to you.'

Alison, an unusual mode of address with her; also her voice and expression went well with the lowering Sunday —the leaden sky, the gloomy unfriendly light. In harmony with this look was her manner, shorn of the acceptable approach or other social fleece; in the pallor and rigidity of her face was no room for anything but determination.

'Of course,' Alison acquiesced. Her first pause of un-readiness, without particular misgiving, was yet leavened with surprise; it came over her suddenly how very little —for quite a number of days—she and her old college friend had spoken to each other at all. In this new reali-zation, as Myra continued to stand silent and implacable, she could do no better than offer, 'I was going to the front.'

'All right,' said Myra, and together they left Mowbray's, walking in silent rhythm to the promenade, which wel-comed them with the customary blast in their faces.

'This is no good,' Myra announced curtly, and led the way to a shelter. Within this pleasureless little pleasance of flimsy wood and glass the wind-roar was diminished and its lashing tamed to occasional swoops; the moment they were settled Myra turned upon her a face of un-qualified demand and began, 'See here: what you're working on at the library—it's nothing, actually, but the stuff that old Miss Tollemache left us, isn't it?' The ques-tion was delivered like a bullet, with a bullet's momentum behind it of stored-up grievance. 'There's no mystery about it for God's sake, it was in the local rag. It *is* the Tollemache bequest—?'

'Yes,' acquiesced the other, genuinely at sea.

'And nothing beside? I mean, no Norman French or Saxon English mixed in with it? it's nothing but the usual country-house library dating from the seventeenth century maybe—?'

'That's all.'

'Then I never heard anything like it, never in my life.' Into the hard glance turned upon her, outrage carved a new dimension. 'When you wrote and told me Durant'd engaged you I thought, well, something's turned up in the Tollemache lot that requires a specialist, or there's something else terribly precious and hush-hush—but you say that what you're working at is no more than the Tollemache odds and ends—?'

'No more than that.' She was still unillumined by any sense of where all this was leading. 'At least so far.'

'Then it's abominable, that's what it is.' Myra sat back, every word striking like darts into a board. '*I* should be doing that work, not you. I've done exactly the same job for the library twice now. Twice!' she threw at the other. 'Did you know that?'

'No,' Alison returned dispassionately. 'How could I?'

'There was no need for Durant to bring in someone from outside, absolutely no need at all,' she pelted on angrily. 'Now if it'd been medieval parchments or Elizabethan script I'd be the last to object, I'm not up to handling that and you are. But *this* muck—just a jumble of papers from an unimportant local family—and to deal with that, Durant drags you in! What for?' Her glare reinforced her voice. 'We've the same qualifications, up to a point. Of course I couldn't afford to go on and specialize,' she accused bitterly, '*you* could,' and broke off short, waiting.

'I hardly know what to say,' Alison began, after a moment. For all that the nature of the attack had been utterly unexpected she spoke without faltering, but slowly and with care. 'All I was told was that the library had received a considerable bequest of papers never classified and in a state of neglect, and would I care for the job. So of course I was glad to say yes.' Ironically it came back to her how much of her pleasure had been the thought of seeing Myra again. 'Other than that I knew nothing of the situation. Obviously you must see,' she appended, 'that I couldn't have known.'

'Oh, I believe you.' Myra's grating voice flung at her, impartially, absolution and condemnation. 'It's not your fault, I never said it was.'

A silence of some moments followed. And whatever filled Myra's silence (thought Alison) her own silence was filled with decision, immediate and sharp. Moreover she had not even been at the trouble of making this decision; Myra had made it for her.

'I'm the senior library assistant, after all.' Beside her the complaint was still unravelling. 'I've been simply ignored—passed over. It'd serve Durant jolly well right if I resigned. Or—' she paused '—lodged a formal complaint with the Governors.'

Alison looked at her curiously, struck by her successive changes of tone. She threatened to resign, she threatened an appeal to the Governors, but her impetus of grudge had fallen to bluster, and from bluster to whining. As the other groped among these inconsistencies, Myra said, 'Well, that's all.' Her voice went dead; whether the conviction in it had grounded upon fatigue or some other reef, certainly it had lost all its impact. 'I just wanted you to know the score, as far as I'm concerned.'

She got up and walked off abruptly.

VI

On Monday morning, and for the last time, Alison took her way to the Champernowne Library. Sadness slowed her to a trudging pace and made her eyes chartless with melancholy. As short a time as she had been here she had fallen into a pattern of small pleasant habits; the pleasure of walking in this ancient village with its occasional enigmas—why, for example, should there be a life-sized swarm in painted ironwork over one house, when obviously it could never have been an inn? Then the pleasure of buying her newspaper in the old shop dim with its bottle-glass panes, the civility of the woman who served her, the pleasure of denying herself even a glimpse of the paper, saving it for her tea-break. . . .

By perversity of fate, never backward in giving regret a sharper edge, there was sun this morning, faint sunshine that gilded the morning mists. Goldenly suffused by this pale golden wash, the tranquil Regency streets looked both real and unreal, as if recalled by magic to their pristine freshness—before wavering like disturbed reflections and dissolving once more into the past. Essence of an older England, owing its survival to an angel with a flaming sword—but an angel not immortal, whom time would erase. Then cheapness and greed, as always, would trample in overnight like hogs. . . .

All at once she longed furiously not to go back this soon to London, back to its crowded noisy streets and

bad manners, vandalized like so much else; she longed
to cling for a while to this peacefulness, this testimony
of a thing once acknowledged as unique the world over
—English civilization. Before entering the library she
glanced back the length of the cobbled street with its
double row of enchanting doll-houses, and by the timid
sunlight saw them as defenceless, doomed and aware of
their doom; leaving behind them the only bequest in
their power, an endearing loveliness remembered.

He was in his office; one question in her mind had been
whether he would be there first, or whether she would
have to support the extra strain of waiting for him.

'Mr. Durant,' she truncated salutations a little abruptly,
'may I speak to you for a moment?'

'Of course,' he returned; his disarming readiness she
countered by saying, 'Could we in here, I wonder—?'
and indicating her workroom.

'Yes, of course,' he repeated, yet patently with incomprehension. While he got to his feet she was unlocking
the door; though she preceded him, the effect was as if
she swept him in before her by mere singleness of purpose. She was completely sure of herself, having planned
the interview from first to last. In his office there would
be interruptions, the telephone, the secretary, the assistant. She was determined there should be no interruptions;
that everything should be dealt with in one clean sweep.

'Mr. Durant.' Only dropping her handbag and newspaper on the table, but with no move to take off her hat
and coat, she turned to face him. 'Will you please accept
my resignation, to take effect as from this morning?'

His silence was almost welcome, as being part of what
she had foreseen. Protest, objection, possible resentment,
she was prepared for them all; no argument of his would

find her wanting. Simultaneously she knew she must justify her conduct by the fullest possible explanation, and this she was able to do from the high ground of professional ethic. It was awareness of an irreproachable moral position that made the backbone of her resolute manner.

'I'm very sorry,' she pursued. 'I'm happy here, I love the place and the work and I'm grateful to you for—for making it available to me. But I wasn't aware that—that a situation existed in—in which—' she paused, annoyed at the hitch in her determined fluency '—I was committing a sort of trespass, of course quite unconsciously. If I'd known,' she wound up a little breathlessly, 'I'd never have accepted the work in the first place.'

'You were committing a trespass.' Calmly he had winnowed the grain from the chaff. 'And what, in fact, is this trespass?'

'Well, that actually—that—' For someone who had rehearsed with so much care, she was making rather a hash of it. '—that actually, the same work I'm doing now—was previously done by one of your staff.' Having got this out, she had surmounted the worst of the awkwardness; it only remained now to agree on the period of notice, and she would be clear of the tangle. 'One of your regular staff,' she supplemented, 'if I'm correctly informed—?'

'Quite correctly,' he agreed.

'Well, in that case—obviously it's rather uncomfortable for me to feel that a qualified person has been passed over in my favour.—I found all this out quite indirectly,' she lied, 'from an outside source,' and congratulated herself on her cunning. 'But since you confirm that my—my information is correct, and that I'm treading on someone else's toes, I must ask you again—please—to accept my resignation. Subject to your convenience.' She lapsed gratefully into formula. 'But if you could possibly let me go not later than—next Monday—?'

She ran down and he let her run down, without comment; only now his grim look came home to her.

'Miss Pendrell,' he began formidably; the coldness of his voice matched the coldness of his eyes. 'There are aspects of this situation which I must make clear to you. It happens that our board of Governors have authorized —*very* rarely—the sale of certain items bequeathed to us, at auction.'

He paused; she stood blankly, yet in her blankness sensing, beyond his atmosphere of displeasure, something much more complicated than displeasure.

'Now in all such sales,' he pursued, 'we have been successful—entirely successful—in remaining anonymous. Champernowne has never appeared by name, in any such transaction. And if this anonymity seems to you elaborate hugger-mugger,' he pursued, gaining in harshness, 'let me tell you that with any hint of new bequests, we are literally hounded by dealers. With prices sky-high and climbing you can hardly believe how frantic such people are for saleable stuff, how persistent they are, and what expedients some of them—the less reputable—resort to.'

During his second pause her chief awareness, vague but increasing, was of having taken on more than she reckoned with.

'Now among ourselves, Miss Pendrell, among the staff of Champernowne—' his voice became more and more deliberate '—everyone knows that all library business is confidential, as in any other office. Therefore when you tell me—'

She could hear him coming to the point of his ominous preamble, hardening toward some final . . . . demand? what demand . . . ?

'—that you've heard talk about which member of staff handled which material, and tell me moreover that you've heard this from *outside* the library? you did say from outside—?'

Her lie was being offered to her like a changeling; whether she owned or disowned it, she was trapped.

'—that disturbs me extremely,' he was saying. 'I needn't remind you of recent thefts from museums? art-collections?'

A chill pinioned her, an ice-bound incredulity. Not by several eons of time could she have imagined this development—this sinister burgeoning—of her well-meant lie with its praiseworthy motive, sacrificing her job in justice to Myra. Gaping, she stood in a void and let his voice bludgeon her.

'We ourselves have had two robberies,' he was saying. 'Some things from our museum, not very valuable, but still—! and nothing found out about them. But don't you see, Miss Pendrell—' the exaction of his voice changed to undisguised appeal '—that talk such as you've heard about the library, from outside, must have come from *inside?* And that therefore at best some member of our staff is reprehensibly careless, and at worst is acting as a pipeline in and out, for what can be only one purpose—yes?' He had checked. '—you were going to say something—?'

She managed a sound of negation.

'Well then, if I'm right about the pipeline—' he let fall a brief hiatus '—don't you see how imperative it is, Miss Pendrell, to identify and get rid of it? But how can I find it, other than by tracing it back from this outside source of yours? And even—' he nailed her with new demand '—even if you were told this in confidence—'

'I wasn't,' she croaked, disorganized.

'—I would still be forced to insist on an answer.' He had ignored her interruption. 'To ask you urgently, as a matter of the library's right, for the name of your informant. Failing that—'

He was pressing hard, giving no quarter; *he means business*, reached her cloudily and too late.

'—failing that, I must inform the Governors of my suspicions that some undercurrent exists, some leak. Then it rests with them to call in, or not call in, the police.'

Another qualm smote her, a variation of the chill. Police. Her innocent and creditable falsehood could end with police. . . .

'I've been lying to you.' She capitulated totally and ignominiously. 'Only about one thing, though.'

He waited, impassive.

'I didn't get my information from outside the library,' she bore on. 'I got it directly. From the person who felt she'd been . . . ah . . . supplanted.'

'And this person is—?'

'Miss MacKinnon.'

Of course he had known it beforehand, there could be little mystery about it; she struggled on, feeling singularly exposed and foolish.

'She told me that she'd worked on—on similar acquisitions here, and she saw no reason she should be—well, pushed out—in favour of an outsider. Especially with her qualifications,' she added. 'She was unhappy about it, very unhappy.'

His look, noncommittal, gave her no help; she had to flounder along as best she might.

'And I understand her point of view completely,' she

strove on. 'So you see how—how impossible a situation
—it is for me. I apologize for trying to mislead you—wasting your time—but none of that alters the basic position.
Which is the reason I asked you,' she summed up, 'and
why I ask you now, to accept my resignation. And please,
as—as soon as possible.'

She waited for his acceptance; whether friendly or
unfriendly, he must see that he had no choice.

'Miss Pendrell,' he said; his voice was entirely amiable.
'Would it make any difference if I told you—in entire
confidence—that even if you resigned from the job, Miss
MacKinnon would not be considered for it, under any
circumstances?'

'No,' she returned, considerably surprised but unyielding. 'No, it wouldn't make any difference. You see, it's
also—living in the same house with her and being aware
of her attitude, day after day.'

'But if you lived elsewhere—?'

'There's nothing nearby comparable with Mowbray's,'
she answered. 'And I can't afford hotels.'

'If Miss Carew helped you look—' he persisted.

'No, no—it's too difficult. Uprooting, packing, moving
—too cumbersome. Anyway I'd be seeing her here at
the library, I couldn't be dodging her all the time—running away. No.' Interrupting him she had achieved repu-
diation, complete. 'It's all too complicated—much easier
if I just go.' She offered a deprecating smile. 'So if you'll
just accept my resignation—'

'But I don't,' he returned in the pleasantest voice imag-
inable. 'Accept your resignation is precisely what I'm
not doing.'

'Well!' she said icily, after the moment of shock. Her
eyes hardened, she got her mouth closed again, and stiffened like a ramrod. 'All I can say is that—' she groped

for some crushing retort and failed lamentably to find
it '—I'm amazed, Mr. Durant. I—I must say I'm astonished.'

'Why?' he asked equably.

'Why! because—' she stopped dead from outrage and
the sense of lines unfairly included in the script. 'Because
I've told you why. It's unpleasant for me to stop here,
personally and professionally unpleasant. I call that a
good reason—the best of reasons.'

'I don't for one moment suggest,' he placated, 'that
your reasons are slight or frivolous.' He paused. 'But I
can't consider them sufficient.'

'*I* can,' she retorted smartly, then cursed herself inwardly for the sound of it.

'From my point of view,' he continued, with infuriating courtesy, 'you wish to avoid some personal embarrassment. But this temporary embarrassment of yours,
as against the library's needs, doesn't seem to me enough
of a makeweight. Miss Pendrell—' his voice turned persuasive '—do please try to see our position. Already we're
badly behindhand with our arrangement of new material,
for—for various reasons.' He had hesitated minutely, or
perhaps her impression was wrong. 'And if this stuff piles
up still more, if we're faced with ruinous arrears of classification—'

He gestured propitiation and appeal.

'—you know as well as I do how this demoralizes the
whole machinery,' he summed up. 'Curtails or impairs
our whole usefulness.'

'No,' she said flatly. 'I still can't barge into Miss Mac-
Kinnon's department.'

'Miss MacKinnon has no department,' he said quietly,
'and never has had, but that of senior library assistant
in the public reading-room.'

'I don't care.' Recklessly she threw aside restraint.
'Whether she has or not, she considers she's been shoved
out unfairly, and she's prepared to make my life a misery.
And it's not worth it, that's all, it's not good enough. So—'
she drew a breath, harassed but conclusive. '—so I'm
offering you a week's notice as I said at first, but I—I
must insist that you accept my resignation.'

'And I refuse to accept it,' he returned.

'You refuse—!'

'The library engaged you out of serious need and in
good faith, and I'm holding you to your engagement.
For illness, family emergency, yes, I'd release you.' He
was maddeningly polite. 'For the reasons you've given
me, no.'

Fury silenced her for a moment, and by no means fury
alone; against her will she had to reflect. It was true that
this job was not contractual in the strict sense of the term,
only a matter of correspondence between him and herself. If she simply ignored his refusal and walked out, it
was doubtful—more than doubtful—that he would pursue
the matter legally. All the same, the position was by no
means comfortable. Her reliability was part of her reputation in the world that she inhabited—the small concen-
trated world of archivists and keepers. If in this instance
she flouted an obligation over an employer's protest, the
story would follow her among the specialists on whom
her living depended. And it was a reasonable living, with
more work than she could handle; for this reason her son
could go to good schools and participate in all extra ex-
cursions at home or on the Continent—where he was now,
in fact, on an unusually expensive jaunt. . . . .

These calming considerations did anything but calm
her. A burning heat—in this chilly room—was mounting
from her neck to her face, so much so that unconsciously

she wrenched off her pudding-basin hat and flung rather than dropped it on the table.

'Very good,' she said in a breathless voice. 'V-very good. If that's how you choose t-t-to see it, of course I've no option b-but to—to continue.' Disjointedly she racked her vocabulary for something to scarify him with, and came up with nothing adequate. And he standing there with a composure that not only drove her to boiling-point, but that increased visibly the higher she boiled. 'I wasn't prepared for duress—coercion,' she flung at him. 'I'm unfortunately used to—to civilized treatment. I'm not prepared to cope with this—this miserable quibbling, this letter-of-the-law pettiness—'

She stopped dead all at once; politely he waited till she blew off the rest of her available steam. It took another instant for her sudden rigidity to reach him; her head strangely downbent, her breathing suspended. Wondering what had struck an angry woman in full cry into this marble stillness and silence, as yet puzzled rather than concerned, he took a couple of steps toward her before realizing the ghastliness of her face and staring eyes—fixed on the newspaper that had fallen open as her hat glanced against it and now lay open, screaming in black headlines. SCHOOL BUS IN DEATH PLUNGE, TOR ABBEY CHARTER . . . STEEP WINDING MOUNTAIN ASCENT . . . LIST OF DEAD AND INJURED NOT YET AVAILABLE. . . .

At the instant that his unready eye had swept it came a sound, awful, from deep in the marble image, the naked sound of naked distress from overwhelming shock. All at once the image broke from its violent immobility into violent motion, stammering in an inhuman voice, 'My son.' Mindlessly she had crammed the dented hat sidewise on her head, all the time saying, 'My son, my son.

Chris—!' She took a couple of fast stumbling steps. 'I—
I must go—must find out—'

'Miss Pendrell—' he essayed, for the moment almost
equally demoralized.

'Must—must find out—' with thickening voice she blun-
dered in half-circles like a damaged bug, trying inaccu-
rately for the door.

'Wait,' he urged, grasping her sleeve with one hand
and with the other pushing a button of the house-phone,
by good fortune on the same table. 'Miss Carew, quickly
—next my office, quickly!' All the while he was gripping
her arm against her weak flailings to escape; all the while
she had not stopped babbling, 'Must—must find out. Chris
—must go—must—'

Another sound tore from her painfully, of more ominous import; in the next moment he had plucked off the
hat that was riding her head askew, and supported her
while she was sick over the basin. Miss Carew's racing
footsteps had now impinged on the scene; rapid asides
followed to which she was deaf, also hardly aware that
he had shunted her to the efficient grasp of the secretary
while saying, 'Make her sit down, I'll try to find out—'
As he moved toward the door, the phone had begun
shrilling in his office. 'Oh Lord—!' He disappeared.

'No, Miss Pendrell.' Without trouble Miss Carew restrained the disintegrated creature who saw and heard
nothing, obviously, only continued to thresh feebly
against restraint. 'Wait, wait.'

'Must go . . . must find out . . .'

'Yes, but not like this, you can't go out like this.' She
mopped the other's wet forehead with a matter-of-fact
touch. 'Mr. Durant's trying to find out, he's trying now.'

'Chris,' muttered Alison. 'Chris.' With a long sigh she
seemed to collapse on herself, her head sunk and her face

chalky, a woman young and vital with anger five minutes ago and now shrivelled and old, extinguished. There
followed a considerable pause, infrequently broken by
Durant's voice, half-audible in its extreme brevity and
with long silences in between. All at once a monosyllable
cracked like a whip from the office, followed by his appearance in the doorway.

'Miss Pendrell,' loudly and ruthlessly he plucked the
huddle in the chair from its numbness, staring at her the
while with incredulity, with a sort of awe. 'Miss Pendrell!
It's Chris on the line.'

'Chris—?' she mouthed idiotically, with vacant eyes
and face.

'Hurry!' he urged. 'It's a poor connection, his call came
through mine.'

'Better help her walk,' suggested Miss Carew, taking
an elbow.

'No,' said Alison in a loud unrecognizable voice. Again
violent, she fought off support and fought herself upright
with unnatural jerking movements, like a galvanized
corpse. 'I can walk.' She lurched unsteadily through the
door; from it they heard, 'Darling. Oh darling, Oh darling.'

'Mummy.' The far-away voice was sober, utterly without its accustomed ring and vitality.

'Darling, are you all right? are you all right?'

'Perfectly all right. I've been trying to get through since
last night, but with no phones nearby—then the first run
on them, you can imagine—'

'But you're all right? you're sure you're all right?'

'Oh Lord, yes.' His voice, waxing and waning on the
faulty line, even sounded a little impatient. 'I took a bump
or two, I was lucky. It's nothing.'

'You mean there're . . . badly hurt . . . ?'

'Yes,' he said flatly. 'We ones that could, 've been helping.'

A hornet's buzzing came on the line, a signal evidently; through its obstruction barely penetrated, ''Bye, Mummy, 'bye. . . .'

Still she clutched the phone, listening avidly; there had been no sound of disconnection, nothing, except that he was there no longer. Slowly replacing it, first she became aware that she was sitting in Durant's chair at Durant's desk, and second, that Durant and Miss Carew had appeared hesitantly in the doorway and were regarding her with concern.

'I'm sorry.' Essaying to get up she fell back, then tried again, floundering up by support of the desk. 'Very sorry—'

'Miss Carew will take you home.' He and the secretary advanced briskly. 'Sit down.'

'I'm . . . all right.' Inertly she was allowing Miss Carew to button up her coat, which she must have unfastened in the heat of argument, and with like passivity let her hair be smoothed and covered with the punished hat. 'No, no, I'm all right, I—'

'Take my car, Miss Carew?'

'But I'm quite all right—'

'I'll take mine, I'm more accustomed—'

Ignoring the casualty's bulletins of well-being, they communicated over her head.

'I'll bring it around to the side,' said Miss Carew, and vanished. Upon the office fell a double quiet, hers and his; in the silent regard he bent on her was something more than mere pity—a look of awakened consternation at what he had seen, whose nature he understood too well: the misfortune of a single and dedicated love. . . . *Poor girl,* he thought, where an hour ago he would have thought, *Poor woman*. Then Miss Carew had returned, and together they supported her into the corridor, none of them aware of the figure that emerged from a door behind them, and whose stare followed them greedily down the hall to the staff entrance.

Miss Carew, who did everything excellently, was an excellent driver; she went fast, heading for the empty front and glancing now and then at the shell sitting wordless beside her. On principle disliking any presentable woman who came into the orbit of Thomas Durant, she had reserved for this one a little extra dislike; from her separate room bitterly and daily resenting that cozy nearness to her employer, that innermost room with no access but through his office, that gave endless opportunity for cheerful exchanges and informal friendship, perhaps even more than friendship. . . . Now, looking at the object of envy with its deathly pallor, its streaks of hair unbecomingly plastered on its forehead, for the moment she pitied her enough to forgive her. Deep within Miss Carew herself the memory of the summer of '42 was not so much excluded as buried; something that over the years she had fled in panic. Even now, with this woman's destroyed look bringing back that hell of desolation, she had to sheer away from it uncomfortably. . . . .

'Miss Carew,' struck abruptly on her ear, 'please stop.' At once she braked and turned, prepared to assist during another bout of sickness, and was astonished to see the shell in motion, opening the door and getting out.

'I'm all right,' it was saying, over her outcry of 'No! Miss Pendrell, no, you mustn't—!'

'I'm all right,' the casualty repeated firmly. 'Miss Carew, thank you a thousand times for your kindness—no, I don't want to go home, I'm going to sit for a while on the front, it's just what I need. Then if I'm able I'll turn up again at the library, and if I'm not able—' she overrode a continuing protest '—if I'm not able, I promise you I'll go home and lie down. I promise,' she asserted fervently against the secretary's angry capitulation and her sour, 'I don't know what Mr. Durant will say.'

Standing on the kerb she watched Miss Carew make an expert full circle and drive away.

VII

In her legs was still an airiness, a feeling of alienation
from her body; on these detached appendages she wavered toward the nearest shelter. Then for a long time
she rested immobile, perfectly blank, from time to time
drawing a deep unconscious breath. Before her tumbled
the hostile-coloured sea, restless; the strong sea-wind
brushed her face in irregular gusts, inexpressibly reviv-
ing. The raw briny freshness was making her whole more
quickly than one might believe, yet she continued to stare
before her—apparently at the ocean, in reality down into
the fissure that had opened momentarily beneath her,
and averted her eyes, appalled. Suppose the worst to
have happened, suppose the world to be forever empty
of that one voice like no other voice, suppose herself
condemned to survive in a terror of emptiness lasting
forever, as long as she herself lasted. . . .

Then she upbraided herself for behaving badly, for
having disrupted the morning's work of two busy people,
incidentally making a disgusting spectacle of herself—
and for misfortune not even confirmed, only possible.
Shameful, she must crawl back and apologize for her
cowardice and lack of self-control. . . . . The need to
apologize pushed her into getting up; lethal weakness
dumped her back on the bench, in the same moment
dealing her a hard blow—the knowledge that apart from
Chris she had no life at all: that her life was wholly a

parasite on his life. Bad, like all parasitism; bad and precarious, and there was nothing she could do to change it. . . .

Yet from this dark perception she was lifted, all at once, by a transport and passion of gratitude such as she could never have imagined herself feeling. A passion with no outlet, since she had no personal deity to whom she could offer it; in compensation she applied the lash of self-contempt to her back once more. Her whole life up to this moment had been a matter of gross degrading selfishness and blind exclusion of every other living being. That her dedication was all for Chris, not for herself, absolved her of nothing; her son-worship, in the end, was self-worship. Imbedded in this criminal obliviousness, she had done nothing for anyone as long as she could remember. Quickly she must begin to make up the arrears, quickly find someone, anyone, as receptacle for the gratitude that was bursting her at the seams. . . .

An intrusion; an intruder who sat down in her shelter, at the other end of the bench. Why, why in this particular one, there were plenty of empty ones. . . . She turned vindictive with annoyance, then reminded herself of her moral rebirth a few seconds old, and looked convertly at the newcomer. He in turn was staring seaward as fixedly as she had done earlier, yet a mysterious awareness of her glance produced speech from him.

'Col' day. Nasty col' wind off the ocean.'

'Oh yes, it is,' she assented.

'Feels good to set down,' he pursued. 'Still, when you does, ain't much comfort in these places. Nor much welcome for anybody's arse,' he added darkly, 'in these yere benches.'

'No, there isn't,' she concurred, aware that the portion of her own anatomy so referred to was aching from the cold hard seat; she had been too preoccupied to notice. Meanwhile, and because so far her companion had spoken with only his profile toward her, she was able to observe him surreptitiously—a squat old man, thick-shouldered and slumped; a wornout residue, timeless, of lifetime labour. His hands lay stiff and half-closed atop one another on his heavy gnarled stick; he breathed with the rattle and wheeze of chronic bronchitis; he coughed frequently and unpleasantly. A heavy frayed old cap extinguished his head and ears, a baggy frayed old overcoat, mud-coloured, swathed him from neck to ankles; the tender mouths of this garment, the pockets, had corners darned and redarned and loosening again. And where yesterday she would have escaped at speed from this distasteful apparition, now she waited with actual humility upon his next utterance. If he needed someone to listen she would listen; she must take care, great and jealous care, not to lose any opportunity of amends. . . .

'Three an' fifty year I was porter on our station,' he vouchsafed. 'Till they made away wi' the line—three an' fifty year.'

'Really?'

'Got the prize for the bes' garden, fower year runnin'. Now I draws my railway pension.' He cackled sardonically. 'Fower shillin' an' tuppence a week, what they calls one an' twenty noo pence. Drat they things, never got accustomed an' never will.'

'Oh,' she murmured with concern.

'One an' twenty noo pence a week.' For the first time he turned toward her full face, with coarse white stubble on the chin and old unblinking pale eyes. 'Can't light me pipe in this dratted wind—get the smoke blowin' back in yer nose.'

'It's horrid,' she agreed. 'Wouldn't it be better if you didn't come out in this cold?'

Not answering, again he turned his head toward the wallowing sea always upheaved and tormented by its unseen daemon; surveying it with neutral and comprehensive disgust, he brooded.

'Better if you stopped indoors?' she persisted (or he might have nothing but a doss?) 'At home?'

'I tells you what.' He answered weightily, from depths of profound and immovable conviction. 'Women likes to have their kitchen to theirselfs. The wife she don't want me underfoot with her cookin' an' washin' an' that. So I stops outside till dinnertime. Better that way. Easier.' He relapsed into conclusive silence.

'May I offer you this?' Without distinct intention she had drawn money from her handbag and pushed it between his hands. 'With best wishes?' As he turned his slow regard on her, uncomprehending, she pressed it further into the gripless old fingers, quailing to think of it torn away by the wind and whirling irrecoverably in the distance. 'Have you got hold of it?'

'W-why,' he began mumbling. 'W-why, madam—'

'Thank you, thank you,' she gabbled, and fled. At every stage of her life, not excluding the present, every separate pound in her pocket had had its own separate and painfully distinct identity. But the notes she had thrust into the astonished old hand had no identity nor importance, no existence even; they were a first microscopic offering to the something, the someone that permitted her still to have a son, unlike other unfortunate people in this same moment. . . . .

Shivering she wrenched away from the thought, and for comfort began to calculate. The couple of pounds should give her new friend about two months of a pub fireside with a pint in his hand, instead of a cold bench on the blowy front. Also in two months the weather should have softened a bit. . . . .

She turned off the promenade and at once saw Tim in the distance, coming toward her at a lively clip. On closer range she saw he was holding something and champing at it with evident relish; when she could see what it was, the half-eaten green apple struck her with the same comfortless sense as the promenade shelter, with its cold varnished smell of loneliness. He must be living on sausage-rolls and fried bread and the occasional bit of fruit. She thought of Chris having to make do on such stuff, and her heart contracted. Now he had come up, saluting in his friendly way; by his unconcerned manner she realized, thankfully, that no word of her crisis and collapse had got around the library.

'What a wind!' she offered.

'I like it,' he returned. 'Blows away that library stink.'

'Oh yes,' she agreed. Her maternal solicitude was finding his thin clothes inadequate, yet he seemed comfortable and perfectly pleased with life.

'A few hours in the stacks, and you get that mouldy taste up your nose and down your throat, I'm always glad of an airing. Anyway,' he pursued energetically, 'you've noticed this is a good place for walking?'

'It's very pretty,' she assented, glancing along the curving cobbled street with its period flourishes.

'It's better than pretty.' He brandished the apple-core, rejecting her adjective. 'What I—what I mean—'

'Yes?' she encouraged, as he seemed to grope.

'—it's not one picturesque bit or another picturesque bit, it's the *balance* of the place. From one angle, for instance, a thing looks one way. Then you look at it from a different angle, and it swings about into something so completely different that it knocks you for six.'

'That's an architect's point of view,' she said, interested. 'Are you going to be an architect?'

'Lord no, I might be anything—or nothing.' He grinned light-heartedly. 'All I mean is, whole place is full of surprises. I like surprises.'

'Tim,' she said suddenly. This gangling boy, half-shabby and inadequately fed and by some transference still merging vaguely with Chris, struck so deep a nerve of protectiveness in her that thank-offerings of gratitude were temporarily eclipsed. 'Have dinner with me sometime soon.'

'Golly,' he responded with his irresistible air of welcoming life on all levels, good or bad. 'Thank you, Miss Pendrell, I'd love to.'

'Where, though? I don't know what's hereabout,' she explained. 'What restaurants.'

'Well, there're Chinese places in Hythe and Folkestone—'

'Oh no,' she dismissed the Orient.

'Well, I couldn't say.' Obviously this contingency had never faced him before. 'Hotels maybe?'

'No no, I don't mean hotels. Isn't there any country place anywhere, some good country restaurant?'

'Well, there's the George and Crown at Melhurst.' He regarded her worriedly. 'Real Elizabethan black-and-white. I've never dared go in there, you bet.'

'That sounds more like it.'

'But Miss Pendrell,' he pleaded. 'It must be pricey as hell, I know that old-beams look.'

'So do I, and never mind. Now when—?' she began, and hesitated; reminiscent queasiness of shock hinted that she had better not face an elaborate meal tonight. 'Shall we say tomorrow?'

'Smashing. Thank you, Miss Pendrell.'

'You know exactly where it is? How far?'

'Four miles, about.'

'Well, a taxi—'

'Lord no, I've a—a sort of car. I mean—' he was dubious and apologetic '—I don't know if you'll want to get in, when you see it. But it moves.'

'That's the main thing,' she agreed. 'We'll meet at six-thirty, say?' All country restaurants, she knew, served earlier than city restaurants, and for the best of reasons —staff. 'All right, then I'll book.'

'Golly, the George and Crown—never thought I'd see the inside of that.' He was revelling in the prospect, clearly. 'And don't worry about how I look, Miss Pendrell, I'll be cleaned up and so forth, I won't shame you.'

'I've always wanted to thank you,' she returned, 'for your nice short hair.'

'Oh, that—who wants a lot of hair trailing poetic'lly in the bangers and mash? And look, Miss Pendrell—about the car.' No least awkwardness constrained him. 'You don't want my wreck clanking up in front of where you live, do you? Say I pick you up a few houses away, at that pink one with the bird-cage balcony—?'

'Yes, that's fine.' It was touching how he anticipated details she had not even dreamed of suggesting. 'Spare Mrs. Mowbray's feelings.'

'Cheat the boarders out of something to talk about, too.'

They parted in gay spirits, and she walked on smiling and incredibly uplifted for someone who had come through recent upheaval; and this upheaval remote enough now to make her doubt—almost—that it had happened. . . .

Feeling her strength come back with each step she walked with more and more vigour and entered the library in triumph, considering how ignominiously she had left it.

VIII

She opened the office door; for an instant they stared at
each other in a lacuna of similar duration but dissimilar
content—hers of embarrassment, his of surprise. The luminous pallor of shock heightened her naturally fair complexion to unnatural brilliance, but into this paleness the
ocean air had whipped a delicate apricot; her eyes were
still enormous with the fearful wonderment of having
glimpsed the abyss, her hair was windblown and disordered. Above all she had not had time to assume the
impersonal composure which she wore habitually and
which—he realized for the first time—aged her incalculably
and made her stolid and lifeless. Also in this unmasked
creature was something touchingly defenceless, and
he felt a mingled indulgence and protectiveness; he could
guess how she resented his having helped her in her physical humiliation. . . . This complexity in him lasted no
longer than his first hesitation and his getting to his feet
with, 'You shouldn't, you know, Miss Pendrell.'

'I'm all right,' she averred. 'I wouldn't have come back
if I weren't able.'

'Miss Carew told me you might,' he nodded. 'Not a
very good idea, if I may say so.'

'I'm all right,' she repeated, angry with him for having
seen her breakdown. Disgusting, unbearable . . . 'I'm perfectly able to work.' As she started toward her room he
said, 'Sit down a moment, would you?'

'But I'm all *right—*' she began irritably, and he countered her irritation with a murmur, 'I know, but do sit down.' Only one tone could have evoked compliance from her, and he had used it; not persuasive, not conciliating, only casual. 'For a moment?'

She hesitated, then took a chair and sat bolt upright, staring at him woodenly across the desk.

'I only wanted to tell you,' he pursued, 'that on second thought I consider my attitude of this morning—well—unpleasantly rigid and authoritarian. Possibly because,' he explained, 'your wanting to go took me by surprise, I wasn't ready. But of course if you wish to resign, Miss Pendrell, I accept your resignation. Naturally we can't ask you to remain here if you're unhappy, except that—' he hesitated slightly '—if we can't find a replacement within the week, perhaps you'd consider giving us a few more days—?'

'No,' she blurted. 'I withdraw my resignation.' It came out unwilled and independent of previous intention. 'That is, if you'll let me.' Anxiously she hurried on, impelled by desire to clarify—as much to herself as to him—her change of heart. 'I mean, I—I'm having second thoughts too. If my leaving here won't—you said—do anyone any good . . . or no!' explosively she repudiated the whitewash. 'The truth is, I don't enjoy being pushed around. Why should I let myself be forced to break an agreement? Out of cowardice,' she argued defiantly; some habitual acquiescence in her, some habit of submissiveness, had snapped. 'In order to avoid unpleasantness, just as you said—and you were right, perfectly right. So,' she wound up, not demonstrably in sequence, 'I'd like to take it back —my resignation—if you'll let me.'

'With the very greatest pleasure,' he returned solemnly. 'Thank you, Miss Pendrell.'

A pause fell between them; his hidden smile appeared in spite of him, and at the same moment they both began laughing.

'Well, that's that,' he remarked. 'I'm delighted that you're stopping with us.'

'So am I,' she returned, tried to rise too quickly, and failed—from over-relaxation in her chair; from the novelty (it must be) of feeling completely at her ease with him. Reassembling herself she started to get up once more, and was checked by his next words. 'Tell me about Chris.'

With her bottom an inch above the seat she hovered, then subsided; the invitation was one she had no power to resist. 'I don't want to bore you,' she protested insincerely.

'I shan't be bored.'

'Well—he's almost fourteen. I married at eighteen and he's my—my only child.'

'May I ask—not out of curiosity—' he hazarded '—if you're a widow?'

'No, my husband left me.' Her entire freedom from constraint struck her not then, only later. 'I think he was the handsomest man I'd ever seen. It—it bowled me over completely that he'd take any notice of me. I mean, it was the last thing I expected, I'd never thought of myself as all that attractive. Actually—' she thought a moment '—I understand it less and less as time goes on, his wanting to marry me in the first place. At any rate, we did marry.'

She was silent an instant, puzzled and remote.

'And we'd no sooner married, than he showed what he was. He was half-German, with all the *bad* German qualities in him, and none of the good. That detestable arrogance—conceit, rigidity . . . and his resentments weren't quite sane. He had to dominate you, or you'd better watch out. He had the most beautiful manners if he thought it worth his while to show them, and underneath them this—horrible, beastly—Prussian thing.' Her voice was shaken for a moment; an angrier red lit her cheeks. 'Well, we broke up and he was glad to get out of it—I'd got pregnant straightaway, and he didn't fancy that at all. I've never seen nor heard from him since, thank God, and I got my divorce after three years' desertion and resumed my maiden name. He didn't contest, didn't even appear—and was *that* a stone off my heart!' She laughed shakily, over a laboured breath. 'I'd a nightmare feeling he'd turn up one day and try to claim some sort of rights over Chris, make trouble of that sort—'

'He didn't though, obviously?' Durant soothed. 'Clever of Chris, by the way, to ring you here.'

'Oh, he always knows where to reach me! And when,' she returned. 'He wouldn't waste time trying to find me at Mowbray's, not at this hour.'

'What's he like—Chris?'

She hesitated, then with a sort of shamefacedness opened her handbag, withdrew the snapshot and reached it to him. After this she waited, with downcast eyes and a very faint smile in the corner of her lips.

'Yes,' he said, after a pause. Obviously struck, he continued to scrutinize the boy half-leaning against a wall in bright sunlight; the handsome face, the splendid head with its ruffled crest of hair, the look of intelligence, receptiveness, and less-definable individuality. 'Quite magnificent. Remarkable poise he's got too, for his age.'

'It's absolutely natural,' she defended. 'It's not conceit, he hasn't a shred of conceit. I mean—' she hesitated '—his riding-master told me that Chris was his right-hand man when he'd larger parties to manage. He said–' she hesitated again '–he was a born leader.'

'That's the look he has,' Durant assented.

'And he's so brilliant and so *nice* with it that–that it frightens me. I mean–' she groped '–when anything's that good, you keep waiting for the blow to fall. You're *afraid*–!'

'Don't be afraid,' he encouraged. 'There are a few people who're born complete, and he's one of them, apparently.'

'One child!' Unhearing, she still communed in dire soliloquy with a perpetual dread. 'If only I'd had two or three. . . . Still, I don't believe that having other children makes up for the loss of one particular child.' Her haunted eyes questioned the proposition. 'I don't believe it makes it easier, not at all.'

'Tell me,' he recalled her. 'What's Chris going to do? What's he intend to make of himself?'

'Well actually–'

He had been successful; from fear she had returned to pride and hope.

'–so far, he doesn't seem to have any one great interest. But about a year ago a man from the Home Office came to see the headmaster.' She preened, for all her obvious effort not to. 'Just to talk about Chris.'

'Well! If he's already attracted that sort of notice, I expect you needn't worry.'

'No, very likely not, I–' She checked all at once and jumped up. 'Sorry, I hadn't meant to go on and on–take your time like this. Thank you for everything, and now I'll get back to work.'

'Tell me,' he halted her brisk movement. 'It's of no importance, but your Christian name is Alison, I believe? but Miss MacKinnon calls you Bally–?'

'Oh, that!'

She had the most charming laugh; he had never heard her laugh before.

'That's from Somerville days,' she was explaining. 'When I used to sign myself B. Alison.'

'B for—?'

'Bettrys.'

'Bettrys? Welsh for Beatrice?'

'Yes. You've noticed my surname, of course—my father had a mild passion for old Welsh names. But it looks so affected—Bettrys! I just dropped it, in the end.'

'Like my own first name,' he concurred. '*My* father's antiquarian passion for old spellings led him to afflict me with N-i-a-l-l. Now if he'd been content with plain Neil, I'd have kept it. But Niall! too strenuous by half. So I keep it dark—like you.'

'Just as well, too,' she murmured.

In her chilly retreat she felt the most absurd light-heartedness—double light-heartedness actually, and all from the same source. By nature reticent, knowing how violation of this reticence produced in her only discomfort and embarrassment, she found it astonishing that she should open up so freely and so completely to a stranger, and more astonishing that she should experience from this catharsis not the customary regret, only a headiness—an actual exhilaration—of release. And above and beyond all this was the pleasure of being, for the first time, friends with him; the heart-lifting sense of being friends was such as to compensate, almost, for impossible dreams and longings.

Why should he look at you, after all, she put to herself cheerfully, *if he were free a hundred times over?* and dug into a heap of bundles that proved to be mill- and threshing-house inventories, of a paralyzing dulness.

'What in the world was wrong with you this morning? What happened?'

'Nothing happened.' Unexpected that Myra should latch onto her going home, so soon after the considerable rift between them; striking proof of how slickly her resentments yielded to curiosity. 'I felt a bit wonky, that's all.'

'That's all? It happens that I got a glimpse of you being supported out.' Myra bent a derisive look on her. 'You looked a damned sight worse than wonky, mate—you looked a roight mess.'

'It couldn't have been that bad,' Alison fended, with a moment of sharp dislike.

'Did you come all over queer, ducks?' the hoarse Cockney-burlesque continued, after a checked and offended silence.

'I sat on the front for a while, and it passed.' Alison, murmuring placidly, indulged the hope that her placidity was infuriating.

'Well, I'm glad it was no worse.' Extorted from Myra perforce, this was tantamount to defeat; better yet, her bafflement was virtual guarantee that neither the cause nor the extent of her breakdown had got beyond Durant's office. With unchristian glee she noted that Myra—now wanting to get ahead of her or drop behind—was constrained by their natural equality of pace to remain abreast. For the rest of the way home they neither looked at nor spoke to one another.

'We shan't be seeing much of Thomas Durant at dinner from now on,' said Mrs. Lees-Milburn as they sat down, 'or I miss my guess.'

'He *is* away a good deal,' Alison agreed with polite uninterest and a painful leap of her heart at the name; the remark had been addressed solely to her.

'He'll be away still more, till a certain sad event,' predicted the oracle with portentous relish. 'He'll dine with his father every evening—till it's no longer possible, in the nature of things.'

He'll be with his father some evenings, her fellow-lodger dissented wordlessly. *Not all evenings.* Then her desolation at this absence merged with her first awareness of another absence. Durant was not there, but neither was someone else.

'Seems to have gone, thank God,' Myra offered rather surprisingly, observing the direction of her glance. 'For good, let's hope.'

'Mmmm,' said Alison in spiritless concurrence. That the overture might be construed as a peace-offering was overlaid by her flatness of disappointment. Arriving home with her current of good-will channelled in full spate toward Marcus, she was brought up short by the empty seat; saddened and acutely shamed. Her frequent rejection of his conversational essays accused her of barbarity, no less; too late now to repair her prejudice and inhumanity, too late . . . still, what if he had rejected her tardy gesture with the contempt it deserved? The conviction that he would have done so cheered her up illogically, and her homeless dove flew on with its olive-branch, seeking another ark. Her penitential program, so far, was turning out pleasurable to herself; from this stigma of pleasure she must cleanse herself at all costs. The next target she aimed at was free, surely, from the remotest context of pleasure . . . ?

Yet the intention, when she came to think, was by no means so simple of achievement. One word misjudged, one nuance of charity, would be fatal; the old woman's perceptions were as menacingly alive as a charged wire, and a gauche invitation must invite a savage refusal. Leading up delicately was a first imperious requirement; complete absence of bystanders a second. . . .

And here and now in the wake of after-dinner coffee, with the reduced population guaranteeing more solitude than usual, was her opportunity; the chance she had been waiting for, and through nervousness she was letting it slip. . . . .

'Mrs. Lees-Milburn,' she essayed too abruptly. 'Don't you find that one gets tired of always eating in the same place—I mean, always having dinner at home?'

'Fed to the teeth,' the other barked. 'Nauseously. Still, nothing for it.'

'Well, I'm dying for a little change myself, but I wouldn't go out alone,' Alison ventured. 'It would be so kind of you to have dinner out with me one evening? I mean, if you'd care to—?'

'Adore it,' said Mrs. Lees-Milburn with the speed of lightning. 'Simply adore it. When?'

'You know the places here, I don't.' Wounded sensibilities, she jeered inwardly; if the old lady's acceptance had been a springing trap, it would have sliced her in two. 'Where would you like?'

'The Splendide—Folkestone,' returned the other with the same promptness. 'Big place with a bit of life, even off-season.'

'Very good, shall we say—' Alison paused; dinner with Tim tomorrow, it was shaping up for an expensive week. '—shall we say next Friday?'

'Saturday,' came the instant decree. 'Livelier over the weekend—gayer.'

Dearer too, Alison contributed in silent postcript. *Everything dearer.*

'Dance band and so forth,' the old woman was saying. 'Sit in the ballroom after dinner—have a brandy and watch the dancing a bit.'

'Lovely.' Alison winced slightly; whatever might be said of Mrs. Lees-Milburn, her ideas of pleasure were not on the cheap side. 'Saturday then, and we'll arrange the time later?'

A relief to have got the invitation well over, and above all without an audience—and just in time too, she thought smugly, hearing someone open the door behind her.

'Miss MacKinnon!' the beldame greeted the newcomer, with spiteful triumph. 'Miss Pendrell has asked me to dine with her at the Splendide on Saturday! Isn't that *lovely* of her?'

'Lovely.' Myra's dulcet echo somehow managed to combine venom for the invited with mockery for the inviter. 'Absolutely lovely.' She settled down with a magazine, leaving Alison to reflect on the peculiar malignity of circumstance that had brought Myra—Myra who was hardly ever seen here—into the lounge at just the moment when asking a freak to dinner must tar herself with the brush of eccentricity. The general bad luck of it partly obscured her sense of the old woman's promptness in rubbing Myra's nose in the invitation, and obscured even more her sense of Myra's talent for incubated reprisals.

IX

The sight of Tim and his chariot waiting at a discreet distance made her want to laugh aloud, it was so absurdly clandestine—as if she proposed to start an affair with a teen-age boy, instead of proposing to stuff him to the ears. Still—the thought nudged her furtively—just as well that he waited where he did, and just as well that the day verged on gloaming.

'Good evening, Miss Pendrell,' he greeted her. Even through the greyness an unwonted polish shone about him.

'I warned you,' he deprecated, gesturing at the mass beside him; it was murmuring hoarsely, its sides appearing to heave rather than vibrate. 'Sorry about the torn hood.' He helped her in gallantly and went around. 'Never cared if it rained in on me, but with you . . .' His various manipulations had released a sound as of metallic disembowelment. 'So I've stuck it together with tape, I expect it'll last the evening.'

She started giggling, then the earlier laughter got the best of her.

'It'll get us there though.' He was laughing too. 'If you don't mind being roof-rent.'

'Not a bit,' she assured him with truth. Never since college days had she been in one of those wrecks that kept moving by some miracle known only to its owner; it returned her all at once to being young, light-hearted, and confident of happiness. Glancing at him and seeing his eyes fixed unswervingly ahead, attentive to the un-lighted narrow road and the death-trap turns around high hedges, she refrained from talking to him and set-tled down, instead, to enjoy her well-being. And to savour, also, its ingredients: nine hours of unbroken sleep last night, healing sleep after cataclysm; Chris on the phone again, this time safe in England; her cautious abstinence at table for twelve hours, whose reward she was now feeling pleasurably. . . .

"I hope you're hungry,' she offered.

'I could eat a horse,' was the pleasing answer, and the car seemed to go a little faster. The sea-fog, thinning as they turned inland, still veiled the countryside with a dreamlike quality, the dim look of old prints; by the fitful road-lighting of villages, quickly gone, she glimpsed thatched roofs, a Saxon church-tower, a huge archway cut in ancient massive boxwood. And always the recur-ring horror: that the sight of such things no longer evoked pleasure, only the frightening thought, *How long can all this last . . . ?*

They were clanking into the well-lighted car park of a big Elizabethan house, fine black-and-white. 'Would you like a drink first?' she asked as they crossed the court.

'If you don't mind,' he answered frankly, 'I'd rather eat.'

'So would I. But you're sure you don't want a cocktail, you're more than welcome if you do—?'

'They just take off the edge,' he assured her. Accord-ingly they passed through the lounge with its blazing log fire, then up to the first floor with its own lounge, fireless and much less cheerful; the downstairs one was closely packed, the upstairs one almost empty. And yes, the house was no replica but formidably Elizabethan; to pass into the restaurant they had to duck, not through a door, but beneath a massive wooden screen of two-foot timbers leaning at an angle and perilously low. Walking through she could just feel it graze her hat, and guessed how Tim must have to stoop to keep from dashing his brains out.

It was wonderful to see him eat; as if it were Chris she was stuffing, a thinner version of Chris. And how nice he looked, in contrast with his dusty scruffy look at the library; his fair scrubbed skin, his dark-blue suit by no means new but passing by candle-light; his shirt and collar spanking fresh and crisp and his subdued tie a concession (she felt sure) to her advanced old age. Unexpectedly, marooned with her at this small table, he turned out to be rather diffident, and by some divination she felt this not to be shyness, only the fear that his sort of talk would bore her. She found this touching, and peacefully she acquiesced in their frequent silences. Let him warm up at his own gait and in his own good time; she felt no inclination whatever to prod him into duty conversation.

'Golly, that was terrific.' He had worsted a massive entrée, having previously demolished a plate of hors d'oeuvres sufficient for two if not three. 'Sort of a red-letter day, getting outside of a steak like that.'

'Have another,' she urged recklessly.

'Oh no!' He was genuinely shocked. 'No thank you, Miss Pendrell, that *would* be playing the dirty on you. Anyway, there's still dessert.'

'Have it if you want it,' she murmured, then saw that his attention was elsewhere.

'D'you know—' his voice was cautiously lowered, his face mischievous '—those solid bods over there haven't spoken to each other since we've been here?'

Alison glanced inconspicuously at the middle-aged couple, their faces not less suety than their bodies.

'I expect they've said it all,' she suggested. 'They've had plenty of time.'

'No ma'am,' he demurred, respectful but firm. 'They've never said it because they've never had it to say. And those over there—' discreetly he indicated another couple, a sporting vacuous young man and a stylized vacuous girl '—are just the same, absolute double zero, and don't tell me *they've* had time to say it all.'

'You've been noticing,' she said, amused.

'I always do,' he admitted frankly. 'I always notice and I always listen. Suppose I decided to be a writer, it'd come in no end useful. I mean it's fascinating,' he explained, 'how you get these—these split-second flashes on people's feelings and situations and so forth. And lots of times,' he regarded her solemnly, 'they're not a bit what you'd expect.'

'Yes, people can be so unexpected it shakes you,' she concurred. 'So you think you'll be a writer?'

'Maybe not,' he protested. 'How do I know I'll be good enough? It's too soon. Just now I'm crazy about being alive. And about finding out all I can—I don't care what. *Every*thing's wonderful. What I'm afraid of actually—' again he was solemn '—is safety.'

'Safety—?'

'I don't want it,' he declared like an article of faith. 'Not yet. Safety's being in my step-father's law-stationery business. I can't feel passionate about it, so of course they're down on me, he and my mother both. What I like now is just—just knocking about from one job to another. Getting all I can out of one place, then going on to the next. Now this one—'

At last he was well away and at ease.

'—this library job, I expect I've had it, just about.'

'You're leaving?' she asked, with an unexpected pang.

'Well, not yet. I wouldn't just walk out on old Dur—I mean *Mi*ster Durant—till he'd definitely got someone else. I'd want to be fair, he's always been fair. I mean, absolutely.'

'I see.' She repressed a longing to pursue the topic of old Durant, and thought instead that this boy was by no means so naive and defenceless as he had seemed; he was tough, tougher than Chris—who was tough in his own way, she had no doubt, but differently. . . . 'Yes, a writer would have to listen,' she harked back, for dearth of new ideas. 'To get the rhythm of people's talk, and—and so on.'

'Rhythm—and lots more,' he agreed. 'I mean, supposing you overhear something—just a snatch—and it sounds like a . . . a mystery, sort of. Well, you try to make up the missing parts, fit them in. It's fun, and maybe good practise—stretched the old loaf a bit.'

'I expect.'

'Why, even in this mouldy old library, where you'd never expect—' his enthusiasm broke off; he looked at her alarmed. 'Please don't think I eavesdrop, Miss Pendrell, because I don't. It's just what I can't help hearing.'

'Of course,' she reassured. 'A mystery, you said? in Champernowne? what mystery?'

'Well . . .' He stopped short again, this time uneasily. 'It's just theory after all, my own theory, but— Oh blast, I'd better keep my mouth shut.' Plainly regretting the gambit, he burlesqued feebly, 'Tain't for us toads t'be talkin' about they gentry.'

'Well, all right,' she smiled, intrigued and mildly disappointed. 'You mustn't if you'd rather not.'

'Oh, no it's jolly interesting, I'd like to discuss it with someone—compare impressions. I've never mentioned this before to a living soul.' He stopped again, invisibly trammelled. 'But if it involved someone on upper staff—'

'You needn't mention names.' Her murmur, casual, dissimulated sudden gross curiosity, flagrant encouragement, and—above all—the tide of prescience that his hesitancy brought flooding over her. He had something to tell that concerned Myra; she not only knew it by instinct, but knew it also for something that would connect disconnected threads—Mrs. Lees-Milburn's unflagging virulence, Myra's jealous anger at being supplanted in the library, her variable angers—and knit these things into a more cohesive whole. Also there came back on her, as if she heard them for the first time, Durant's words: *Even if you resigned from the job, Miss MacKinnon would not be considered for it, under any circumstances . . .* With a shock of realization she saw, for the first time, how those words invested Myra with a foggy comprehensive distrust. Worst of all perhaps, did they mean that she continued at Champernowne in the anomalous position of being suspect, but with no sufficient proof against her—?

'Lord no, I'd never name names,' the boy was protesting, during the instant that filled her imagination with crowding obscure shapes. 'I'd never do that.'

'You must do exactly as you like.' Shamelessly giving him, with her indulgent neutrality, the encouragement he was obviously dying for, she had also cast the die on her own account. Since he had not the least idea of her old friendship with Myra nor of their present strained relations, let him talk as he liked; no harm seeing in what direction his conjectures might tend, and after all it might be something utterly different from what she anticipated.

Give him his head for the moment; wait and see. . . .

'Well . . .' Another hesitation, and he plunged; simultaneously they surrendered themselves—he to the luxurious theorizing of the born raconteur, she to the vulgar pleasure of gossip—for whose vulgarity, moreover, she gave not a damn.

'Well you see, it's like this.' He had settled down for an extended effort. 'The library basement's the size of China, more or less. Enormous, the stacks're only half of it, and the funny things down there you'd hardly believe—disused wine bins for the Governors back in Nelsonian days, and a kitchen with one of the first steam-tables—'

'Yes, I've seen part of it.'

'—all those little crooked passageways, you could get lost in them for a month of Sundays. And a million little holes and corners off them, all sizes—and I've taken over one of them. For my own hideout, in fact.'

She nodded receptively.

'I bought a hundred-watt bulb and carried a wire in—stealing current, but not much—and then I pinched some stuff out of an old store-room full of broken chairs and dried-up leather cushions—and I've furnished it a treat, hung some old velvet curtains inside the door so no light gets out. And I keep some biscuits in there and the odd bottle of pop, and when the weather's foul I just have a lie-in during lunch, and read, or sleep—'

'Very good idea.'

'Well, I knew you wouldn't give me away.' He grinned flatteringly. 'At any rate, there's also the librarians' regular common-room in the basement, with a kettle and so forth—'

'I've seen that too.'

'Now, the librarians.'

A new caution—a tendency to pick and choose his words—slowed him perceptibly.

'There's the senior library assistant in the public reading-room and three assistants under her. Then as well, there're a couple of—junior librarians, apprentices or something you'd call them—? Just a couple of silly birds and pretty new to it, I expect. Well, and apparently these kids don't like using the common-room any more than yours truly. And so, to my horror—' he stared despairingly '—they've set up housekeeping a few cubicles away from mine. And talk in there nineteen to the dozen—and don't keep their voices down, I promise you.'

'I see.'

'Well, you do, don't you?' he appealed. 'See my position? Of course I could've given the tactful gentlemanly cough to warn them, but that means *my* hideout's blown straightaway, don't you see? just when I'd got it so nice? So I lay low and kept thinking, Oh hell, they'll go away, it'll be too uncomfortable for them in the long run. But no such luck—they'll go in there and natter three and four times a week. Mostly nonsense of course, but you should hear them on the subject of—'

Again he broke off, looking at her with patent anxiety.

'Miss Pendrell,' he petitioned. 'I don't want you to think I'd talk even this much if I were permanent here, I don't care how small the job was. I'd keep my mouth shut in that case—like any staff should do about where they work. But I'm not a permanent, I'm passing through. And besides, you're the only person I've mentioned this to—I've told you that.'

'Of course.' With additional falsehood and connivance she added, 'Especially since I'm new here myself—and temporary—and wouldn't know whom the juniors meant —or whom *you* meant, for that matter.'

'That's so.' Brightening as his scruples were removed, he launched himself again. 'Well, according to these kids, a certain member of staff isn't exactly popular. Nobody likes her and she likes nobody, according to them. But what had them really steamed up, a couple of months ago, was this person's going up to London and coming back with a lot of new clothes.'

His audience of one jumped invisibly. He was hewing closer to the line than she had foreseen, and moreover she discovered in herself a hundred reasons for not checking him. The undertow of allusion perpetually swirling about Myra; she was sick of it, starving for some light in the vagueness, even the muddled light of conjecture. And she was *not* actually of Champernowne, she was a stranger passing through. Speciousness by all means, yet she could not have stopped him now if her life depended on it. Again she poulticed her conscience with the boy's ignorance of her friendships and estrangements equally; he could never suspect she knew whose identity he was trying to conceal . . .

'Now this happened,' Tim pursued, 'shortly after we'd had a lot of old books dumped on us, from some middling-stately home or other.'

Again her pulse leaped with the same stabbing excitement as at her first pre-knowledge.

'I know that for sure,' he was explaining, 'because I'm the poor clot that loads all that mouldy old stuff in and out of the van and carries it to where you're working now—because it'd all have to be sorted out—?'

'Gone over,' she agreed, 'very carefully.'

'Well, that's just it. Those little nits downstairs seem to connect this person's trip to London—with her having done that lot of old books, just before.'

He paused; it took a full moment before it sank in.

'You mean,' she gasped, 'you mean they think that—that this person—*stole* a valuable book from the collection, and disposed of it in London?'

'That's what they're silly enough to think, those yobs.' He was indulgent. 'Of course they're wrong.'

'Of course,' she snapped. 'Too bad those little idiots can't be given a talking to. Steal books, indeed!'

'Not books,' he demurred.

'Did they ever hear of libel?' His mildness had distracted her, for the moment, from the fact of his disagreement. 'Why, the person might have had some money left them, or—'

'Oh, I expect not, Miss Pendrell,' he opposed her respectfully. 'According to them this person's always trying to impress people, throw their weight about and so forth. If they'd had that kind of good luck they couldn't wait to rub people's noses in it.'

'But . . . .' she groped, completely at sea. '. . . you yourself said not books. But in a library, what else is there to steal?'

'Certainly never books, unless you want to be up to your neck in trouble.' He was firm, and seemingly surprised at her artlessness. 'I understand that lots of the stuff we get's never been catalogued. But supposing you'd pinched something choice, and then a catalogue did turn up? A nasty position for you, not?'

In continuing mystification, she could only goggle at him.

'Or maybe there's a bookplate,' he continued. 'Points straight back to where it came from, and you can't gouge it out without damaging the book. Also—if you're trying for a price—you won't take it to a dealer, you'll put it up at auction with a reserve on it, you've got no other choice.' He gazed at her with calm ascendancy. 'I've worked awhile at Sotheby's, you know.'

'Goodness! that too?'

'Oh, just as a porter—lower than dirt. But talk about fascinating! Golly, I loved it.' He was rapt. 'I love that atmosphere of old things. Actually, d'you know, I almost took a job in this place with a Major Grant, a nice old boy that's got an antique shop near Hythe—Oh hell,' he broke off in apology, 'I've gone way off beam. But what I was trying to say—a book's dangerous, it can leave trails leading back. Nor could you flog it at auction and remain all that invisible. Not,' he informed her with calm sapience, 'if any trouble developed—investigation and so forth.'

'Well then,' she challenged impatiently. 'If you can't sell it, what *do* you do with—'

'Miss Pendrell,' he interrupted on a plaintive note. 'I'm just imagining, I told you—it's just how I've worked out the story on my own.'

'And how,' she demanded transfixingly, '*have* you worked it out?'

'Well, my guess would be—stamps.'

'Stamps?' she echoed blankly.

'People leave letters in books, don't they, and forget them? or maybe just empty envelopes, for a bookmark?' He surveyed her with undeveloped triumph. 'Suppose someone were sorting old books and found something like that with a really valuable stamp on it? Some early issue, very rare, or even practically unique—?'

'Yes, but what about—'

The game began to amuse her; she entered into it with zest equal to his, pitting herself against the problem.

'—what about the address on the envelope?' she objected. 'The family that's owned the books? That gives you away, doesn't it, as much as a bookplate?'

'It might've been addressed to a visitor,' he countered easily; obvious that he had given the matter a lot of thought. 'Or staff, what about staff? I've humped books out of kitchens—housekeepers' books, still-room books. Mightn't the cook stick a letter in there till she'd time to answer it? or some other servant?'

'I expect so,' she agreed slowly.

'So in that case, how do you prove where the envelope came from? How does anyone know?'

'They don't,' she murmured, bemused.

'They can't prove one damned thing,' he asseverated. 'So that's how I've worked out where this—this person —got her glad rags from. From overhauling old books and finding an envelope, maybe more than one, with valuable stamps. And getting a jolly good price for them.'

'It's possible,' she conceded, then qualified hastily, 'As a theory, I mean.'

'You bet it's possible. Moreover, it stands up. It's the only explanation you can't punch holes in.' His eagerness was not a gossip's, only a puzzle-solver's. 'Also someone like that selling it—someone well-educated—they'd know about the value, wouldn't they?' he concluded in triumph. 'Wouldn't they know more about it than ordinary people?'

'I believe you'll end up as a writer after all,' she teased gently. 'You've a turn for—for arrows pointing here and there.'

'Well, if even those kids in the basement could smell a rat . . .' He shrugged. 'I mean, it does seem to add up, doesn't it? to something funny, sort of?'

During their orgy of scandal he had demolished a generous slice of apple pie topped by a tennis-ball of ice-cream; now, with coffee, came the usual basket with its delicate medley of *friandises,* glacé fruit, miniature meringues, petits fours and mints.

Departing, they passed with overfed gait through the upstairs bar, again exhibiting in its dusk a few couples seated far apart. In the duskiest and farthest corner of all she saw, unmistakably, Myra; Myra in absorbed conversation with—also unmistakably—the vanished Marcus. At once everything in Alison went tight with her frantic desire to shrink, to get out of the place unseen and quickly, quickly . . . as if the violence of her wish exerted some sort of magnetic pull, Myra raised her head sharply, with warning. Across the wide spaces of the room, she and Alison looked at one another full—full and incontestably.

'I cabbaged one of those wedges off the cheese tray,' Tim reported with satisfaction. 'Come in handy for my pad.'

'I stole some mints and things,' she returned with equal complacence. 'For my landlady.'

They pulled up at the same discreet distance from Mowbray's, and he turned to her. 'Thank you, Miss Pendrell,' he said fervently. 'It's been wonderful, you don't know how wonderful it was—I'm just sorry I talked you to death.'

'You didn't, it was fun,' she said with equal fervour. 'More fun than I've had in ages.'

Letting herself in, she thought with relief that Tim had

obviously not seen what she had seen at the George and Crown.

It was not quite ten, but the silence was unbroken; in the house it felt late, enormously late. Yet by venturing to open the door of the service passageway she was pleased to see, at the end of it, a line of bright light under the kitchen door. Behind it was another total silence, yet no one could be there at that hour but Mrs. Mowbray; she could present her larcenous booty now, before it lost its bloom. Rapidly she turned out the paper napkin and assured herself she had selected good travellers, glacé fresh grapes and pineapple, tiny macaroons and pistachio in chocolate; she had known better than to risk whipped-cream slices or frail meringues. Pleased with her expert thievery she went down the passage with no feeling of trespass in this kind informal house; it was even known for guests to make themselves a late cup of tea in the kitchen, though this privilege was treated with great respect.

She opened the door gently and noiselessly; the gentleness she had intended, the noiselessness not. The scene in the brightly-lit kitchen was ordinary, revealing only Mrs. Mowbray standing with her back to her. Yet about this back was such a curious tension, about the woman's whole posture such unnatural stillness, that it checked the intruder on the threshold of the room and on the threshold of speech, equally. Simultaneously with this double halt, the rigid back contorted into a spasm—a convulsion almost—of violence. Mrs. Mowbray had been holding, invisibly, a teapot; this she flung at the wall suddenly, with all her strength. At Alison's involuntary gasp she spun around, revealing a pale disordered face, unfamiliar. Following the crash they stared at each other in silence, till

the landlady's broken words indicated returning sanity.
'I'm sorry—' she attempted. 'Sorry, sorry—'

Alison came forward swiftly and half-led, half-
compelled the other into a chair at the kitchen table. 'Sit
there,' she said equably. 'I'll make tea, I'll find everything
—be quiet, don't move.'

Mrs. Mowbray obeyed, to her relief; till the kettle
boiled she sat wordless and passive, with a look of bewilderment. Waiting for the tea to draw Alison came hesitantly to the table and hesitantly deployed her offerings,
afraid that their idiotic frivolity might be—to this woman
harrowed by unknown causes—an incitement to further
hysteria. But Mrs. Mowbray only regarded the bits in
their coquettish paper frills with a desolate smile. 'A
treat,' she said, 'a little treat,' and it was hardly definable
that the word *treat*, in that sad voice, should bring Alison to the verge of sudden tears.

'I stole them,' she explained, fighting off the weakness.
'From the George and Crown.' She poured tea and sat
down; they sipped the scalding amber during a long
silence. Mrs. Mowbray was the first to break it.

'I'm sorry,' she repeated, by her tone still far from recovered. 'So sorry—'

'For God's sake don't apologize,' her guest overrode
her. 'Yesterday I made the most horrible scene in Mr.
Durant's office because I thought my son'd been in that
bus thing, that—that mountain accident.' Her humiliation
that she hated and longed to forget now appeared as a
Godsend, perhaps a healing balm to this woman's trouble,
whatever it might be. Poor Caroline with her benignant
calm, her unchanging dignity; painful to see her robbed
of it like this, brutally stripped. . . .

'I carried on like a lunatic,' she continued spreading
the emollient of her greater shame on the other's un-

known lesion. 'Lost my breakfast and so forth. I had an audience, too—poor Mr. Durant, then Miss Carew.'

'I don't wonder,' said Mrs. Mowbray. 'You had every reason.' She drank more tea, her composure obviously returning. 'Thank God it was you that saw me make a spectacle of myself, and not someone else.' Her faintly-smiling face was her own again, not a stranger's. 'With you I don't mind, somehow.'

'I'm glad,' Alison acknowledged the high compliment.

'Only it's been one of those days,' the older woman pursued. 'Of course I was a fool to take in that man Marcus, even at Myra's special request—' She checked guiltily. 'Oh dear, I wasn't supposed to mention that.'

'It's forgotten,' Alison assured her impassively; the news startled her much less than it might have done earlier. 'No fear.'

'She did press me though,' Mrs. Mowbray persisted in exculpation. 'She said it was business and very important to her, I'd be doing her a great favour and so on. Well, I didn't care for his type very much but she's been with me a long time and I wanted to oblige her—'

'Of course.'

'So I agreed. And he went day before yesterday and left his room in such a state that the cleaner had a tantrum, then it turned out that he'd blocked the basin with something or other and I had to ring the plumber, and it turned out more complicated and expensive than I'd thought—'

'Curse him. But Mrs. Mowbray—' Puzzlement bent Alison urgently toward her companion and loosened her tongue. 'Didn't it strike you as peculiar that Myra'd get you to take him in, then make a point of ignoring him completely? Didn't it make you wonder?'

'She ignored him—?'

'*And* talked him down, behind his back.'

'Did she? I never knew. Or if I'd noticed, I'd take it for some sudden coolness between them—none of my affair. Now if it were something that affected the tone of the house I'd deal with it straightaway, I promise you. But personal undercurrents I wouldn't know about, I shouldn't want to know. I've enough on my plate without.'

'I believe you,' Alison murmured.

'But that—that awful thing you saw me do—you mustn't think I go about slinging teapots at walls, in the ordinary course.' Distress flushed her fair skin and brought back signals of strain. 'B-but—'

'It's all right, it's all right.'

' but ' She had not ignored the interruption, she was deaf to it. '—this house—you see—my husband and my son, we were so happy here, so *happy*—then when it was all over I couldn't bear to leave, they were still here with me, I *felt* them—and the only way I could continue to stop here was this way, pgs. But every once in a while it comes over me—what are these strangers doing in our house? How dare they? how *dare* they?' She was trembling. 'I think I've got used to it, then all at once I haven't. And it—it builds up and builds up inside me till . . . till I've got to smash something.' She sighed gustily, and seemed to return from a distance. 'So that's what you saw, you poor child. I'm so ashamed, I do apologize—'

'Now I've told you not to.' Alison got up and poured more tea. 'Have one of these silly things, to please me.'

'Aren't they pretty,' said Mrs. Mowbray vaguely, ate a grape and after it, encouragingly, took a macaroon. 'How old is your son?'

'Fourteen.'

'Mine would have been fifty-one. Michael fifty-one!'

Absently nibbling the macaroon, she was incredulous and dreamy. 'He was the *essence* of youngness—attractiveness.' Apparently drained by her outburst she was quiet again, inert. 'Still, I mustn't be ungrateful.' It was soliloquy, addressed to no one. 'I've been lucky with most of my pgs. Major Grant for instance, so nice, no trouble at all . . . he's got an antique shop near Hythe and does rather well, I'd say. . . .'

While Alison undressed she reviewed—she could hardly do otherwise—her curious evening; the jollification with Tim, their exhilarating excursion into libel, and the sudden descent to the shocking paroxysm in the kitchen; above all, the painful self-revelation. Not of her landlady's grief for husband and son, since passing time must have transmuted the wildness of her grief into endurance and remembrance. No, the raw unhealing lesion in Caroline Mowbray was the spectacle of strangers making free of her home as though they had every right to do so; the violation of what had been—among people of her class and generation—a foundation-stone of civilized living. She could come to terms with grief; she could not come to terms with outrage, the daily outrage against privacy. . . .

'I know what *your* Fourth Man is,' Alison addressed her out loud, involuntarily, then cursed Myra for putting the image into her head.

X

The tap at her door next morning was light but peremptory; expecting it, all the same she jerked annoyingly. Over-prompt to open because of her reluctance, she saw in the inevitable visitor the inevitable signs—the pale hard face, the implacable intention.

'I must speak to you.' Myra's voice, low and hurried, was imperious. 'Not in this blasted house—but we must talk.'

'On the way to work,' Alison returned, expressionless.

'That's no good either—' Myra, objecting, changed course. 'Well, all right, but let's start ten minutes early. We must.' Her tension opposed the other's expressionless look. 'We must.'

They left the house together as arranged, but the ten minutes' early start had made her scramble; already resentful of the coercion, she was now exasperated. Methodical by nature and forced to be even more so by her work, she had found long ago that hurry unsettled and disorganized her; she loathed it, except for very good reasons. Now as they marched along in total silence she was aware that Myra glanced at her uneasily from time to time, and took deliberate pleasure in withholding from her the least reassurance of responsive glance or word. *Bitch*, she accused herself. *Still, I'm being pushed about. Why should I like it?*

'Not that way,' Myra decreed, as they reached the usual turning. 'We'll go along the front.'

The curt command stoked the other's irritation; it began flaring into resistance—flared, then died all at once, extinguished by strange acquiescence. Wait, the only sensible thing to do; wait for whatever was coming. Accordingly she obeyed without a word, always presenting a profile whose coldness was just this side of contempt. This was doing its share to demoralize Myra, she knew by instinct, and meanly enjoyed the knowledge.

'One of those,' Myra broke their lethal silence. 'In there.' Her determination, a ruthless force, impelled Alison toward a shelter.

The place could not have been worse chosen—the cold horrid little box recalling the other day's entrapped desolation; hers, the worn-out old man's, and now this further prospect of unpleasantness; perhaps this was even the same shelter, she had no exact remembrance. With a faint qualm of nausea enlivened by animosity she fixed on Myra a blank look, calculated to unnerve, and sat waiting.

'You saw me with that man last night,' Myra plunged at once. 'With that Marcus.'

Alison barely nodded.

'Well, all right, I lied to you about not knowing him, that's obvious. But his getting into Mowbray's was accident, pure accident. I couldn't have foreseen that he'd know about the place—or that there'd be a vacancy, and especially not that Caroline would ever in the world take in that type. I'd imagined he'd stop in Folkestone or Hythe, surely.'

She paused, while Alison reflected on the classic device of mixing truth with lies.

'But since he did get in, and since this was a business thing between us—*completely* a business thing,' she stressed, 'of course we had to keep up the show of not knowing each other. I even talked him down a bit—window dressing, sort of.' She invested a smile, withdrawing it quickly when it failed of a dividend. 'Actually, he's a dealer in old documents, autographs, that sort of thing, and he's heard about that foul old hag's trunk. Everyone in certain circles has heard, I told you. So what he had in mind,' she besought, even more rapidly, 'was just a— a reconnaissance. For instance he thought that if she didn't know the potential value of what she had, and if someone told her, she might be tempted. Or if not then, he might still have an edge on other dealers if . . . if one day she'd *have* to sell. And that's absolutely all there was between Marcus and me, and kindly stop looking at me as though I was a moral leper.'

'I wasn't.'

'You were.'

'This Marcus,' Alison digressed. 'How'd you come to meet him?'

'By accident. Through a friend of mine—an antiquarian.'

Your Major with his antique shop, came a wordless postscript from beside her.

'And there's nothing in the least shaming about it, or dishonest,' Myra was arguing hotly. 'All dealers like that are desperate for stuff, it's getting scarcer and scarcer. And a cache, a big cache of unknown originals—they'll do anything to find an approach, just an approach. And yes, Marcus offered me a very nice little . . . acknowledgment . . . if I'd keep harping—not on *her* collection, but on the value of such things generally, the prices that had been paid recently, the money. Then if she got interested he'd move in quickly—strike while the iron was hot.'

'And did you talk to her?'

'Yes. And put my foot in it.' Myra eyed her with a sort of dismal fury. 'Old sow, she'd always looked down her nose at me, but this finished me completely. I'd dared besmirch Mamma's letters with sordid things like money value—prices—she took it like God knows what, offended royalty's nothing in comparison. And since then she's had it in for me.' Myra's cheeks, even in this cold air, were burning. 'Damned old bitch. But anyway—' she drew a long breath and relaxed, like a runner through the tape '—that's the whole story about me and Marcus. Sinister.' She laughed. 'Deep and dark.'

'Well, it's your affair,' Alison commented neutrally. Her own mind retained the conference in the bar on quite different terms; vividly she saw the two heads close together, their absorption suggestive of much more than casual bonds of interest. 'Anyway, I wouldn't have mentioned seeing you together—I'd no intention of talking about it to anyone, ever.'

'Well, I was sure you wouldn't. I just wanted you to understand, that's all.' Myra's accent, understandably, was relieved. 'Oh! that foul old woman, I could see her break her neck and laugh myself to death. . . .'

Her nuance, now of soliloquy, appeared to signal the end of the interview; Alison started to rise, with a perfunctory, 'All right then.'

'Wait, wait.' The renewed command in Myra's voice tightened on her sharply, like a leash. 'There's something else I must ask you.'

The other woman was on her feet, regarding her companion coldly. Conscious of one thing only—that she could not get away quickly enough from this conversation—she prepared a flat *No*, then to her own surprise failed to say it. What cut her off she had no idea, unless it was Myra's changed look—a *different* look, that held her in a new perplexity. This transformation of look and manner, again, was too complicated for snap diagnosis. Its resolution had a queasy edge of hesitancy, its decision was tainted with unease, and its calculation eroded by her fawning, propitiating air.

'Sit down,' she was appealing. 'Come on, Bally, sit down.'

'I'm freezing to death,' Alison rejoined. 'If you must go on, hurry.'

'I can't talk to a pillar—a *standing* pillar—of righteousness,' Myra complained. 'Please don't be difficult, Bally. Sit down a minute, just a minute.'

Alison's rigid descent to the very edge of the bench indicated, by mere scantness of perch, an equal scantness of tenure.

'Look, about Marcus's plan with that old sow,' Myra began hurriedly. 'All right, I couldn't bring it off, she wouldn't take it from me. But she likes *you*.' She paused. 'You're practically matey, the two of you. Alison, if you went to work on her—carefully—I'll bet anything she'd show you what's in that bloody trunk, or at least say what was in it. If you'd butter her up, lay it on thick—and try for a glimpse of the stuff, just a *glimpse*—'

'And exactly,' Alison interrupted, 'what for?'

'Well, I told you.' Myra hesitated. 'Marcus. He'll pay for information, you know. You for getting it, and me for getting you to get it.'

The other hesitated in turn, between anger and curiosity. Curiosity won.

'What good will that do him?' she demanded. 'She still won't sell, any more than she did before.'

'She will,' Myra contradicted dogmatically. 'This time she'll sell, all right.'

'What makes you think that?'

'Because—'

Myra's response, after a silence and a long indrawn breath, indicated a new gambit of unreserve, for unknown reasons of policy.

'—because she'll have to, pretty soon.' She paused again, selecting her items. 'She hasn't a bean, you know, outside of tuppence a week to live on, something like that. And that fool Caroline carrying her at a loss—I always suspected it, and now I know it.' She drew another long breath. 'It was last Saturday afternoon and the house dead quiet, they must have thought everyone was out— and it just happened that I opened my door in time to see Caroline's back disappearing into Lees-Milburn's room. And all right,' she admitted aggressively, 'I sneaked up to the door and put my ear against it. There're times when you make your own luck, and this was one of the times, and don't bother coming all righteous over me.'

'I wasn't,' said Alison, without expression.

'Not you.—Well at any rate, Caroline was saying she couldn't go on much longer at the present rate, she'd simply have to raise her prices. She said she'd still carry on the old way as long as she could, but she was trying to prepare the old girl for it as much as possible, give her time to scrape up something toward the new expense, or even . . . . give her time to find somewhere else to live.'

'Oh Lord,' murmured the other, appalled. 'Hasn't she anything to sell? jewellery?'

'Hoo!' Myra was derisive. 'Haven't you noticed the frightful junk she plasters all over her dirty dress-fronts? She has had good pieces I expect, that class always did, but you can bet they were sold long ago. Soppy old Mowbray cried when she was telling her,' she added. 'They both cried.'

Another brief silence fell.

'She's worried all right, the old scarecrow.' Myra eyed her companion knowledgeably, with restrained gloating. 'Not that she shows it, you've got to admit she keeps her chin up, but she must be sick with worry. Where'll she go, if she's got to leave here? The cheapest hole in a cheap letting-house? Cook on a gas-ring? She's got by so far, yes, but now it's getting pretty close to the knuckle. So—' arrived at the immutable, she paused again '—if Marcus could get some sort of line on what she's hoarding, if he could hit her with an offer when she's down— she'd have to accept, she'd have no choice. But it would help so much if someone like you—really knowing these things—could give him just a hint about the quality of the stuff. Or even the quantity, any sort of lead—'

Alison got up.

'No thanks,' she interrupted. 'I don't see myself spying on anyone, *for* anyone. Least of all,' she concluded, 'for your friend Marcus.'

She started walking off, and after a moment was surprised to hear Myra in pursuit.

'Bally! Bally!' came her voice in petition, before its owner caught up. 'You needn't go all shirty over it, what for? I mean, what'd I ask you to do that was all that bad?'

Out of surprise again, plus sheer incomprehension, Alison turned her head and regarded her old-time friend. Having by now some vague light on her new misshapenness of character, she had taken for granted the only possible aftermath of their colloquy: Myra's hostile resentment that would keep her lingering sullenly on the bench till Alison had got well ahead; after that avoidance, another mutual avoidance both at Champernowne and at Mowbray's. Instead, here she came running and slightly blown, excusing and protesting all the while.

'Goodness, I wasn't trying to get you to *read* the beastly letters,' she panted. 'All I meant was, did they seem in good condition or were they loose or in bundles or what—'

Alison looked at her again, once more perfectly nonplussed by what she saw and heard, for which she could find no better word than *unnatural.* Myra, by nature vindictive, at this moment must be seething with rebuff. Yet, as if held in counterbalance—her longing to turn nasty as against the necessity of avoiding, at all costs, an irreparable break—she restrained herself. And this calculated restraint, again, was the source of her calculated appeasement.

'But if that's how you feel about it, all right,' she was wheedling. 'I'm sorry, I apologize and I . . . Bally, don't walk so fast!'

'It's late,' Alison returned, and walked faster on purpose. Then she had a conviction that Myra's available self-control had run out, and that any moment now she must offer some reprisal, but what. . . . Events informed her in short order.

'By the way, the kid that was tagging you at the restaurant.' Myra's voice was too casual. 'Wasn't he that layabout we've got in the stacks, a janitor's help or something?'

'Yes, he was,' Alison returned. 'Tim.'

'Heavens, I wouldn't know his *name*, but I thought I recognized him. We've absolute *parades* of those tramps passing through, every few weeks there's another. And

all of them absolutely no good, can't stop long in any
kind of job. So.' Her inflection continued playful, but
there was no playfulness in her eyes. 'You were feeding
one of those—at the George and Crown, no less?'

'No less,' Alison murmured. 'He made me think of
Chris.'

'Sugar-mummy?' Myra suggested dulcetly.

'If you like,' her companion returned with no slightest
change in her face, voice or gait. One behind the other
they passed into the library, undeclared enemies facing
each other across unseen chasms of hostility.

That the episode should chafe her, in retrospect, was
understandable. Less understandable was her vague
feeling of incompletion; of some hanging end in their
exchanges that lurked in her far consciousness and would
not be drawn forward. More irritating still—but even
more vague—was her conviction that if she could lay hold
of this loose end and pull, its unravelling would lead to
something directly pertinent, maybe important. Some
allusion of Myra's, something said . . . or even unsaid,
came to her in a sudden flash, less than illuminating;
the sort of flash that leaves in its wake a deeper darkness. Her hit-or-miss dredging of this darkness, from
which her trawl came up empty, so distracted her from
work that she had to stop; she would think of it later.
On the heels of this decision the puzzle was solved—
illogically, as often—by the appearance of Tim.

As he hefted a box of sermons in octavo calf and vanished, without scruple she abandoned what she was being paid to do, leaning her head on her dusty hands
and boring into the murk—now faintly illumined from
one, no, from two sources. First, from Tim: *I nearly took*

*a job with a Major Grant, an old boy that's got a nice
antique shop near Hythe.* . . . allusion whose signifi-
cance she had failed, at the moment, to grasp. Then after
Tim, Myra disclosing her plans and intentions with elaborate frankness, yet omitting a vital detail. About any decent man's profession, there was no mystery. Yet from the
very beginning she had avoided mentioning the Major's
antique shop; a suppression unnatural then, and now
suspect. Alison, no seller nor buyer in the world of old
things, knew nevertheless that an invisible brotherhood
existed among antique dealers, an unseen chain of information, tips, pointers . . . . with electric suddenness
her mind welded connecting links from Myra to James
Grant, from Myra to Marcus, all of them intent on Mrs.
Lees-Milburn and her trunkful of unknown nineteenth
century, perhaps eighteenth century, correspondences.
Trapped by being observed with Marcus, compromised
by her concealment of the antique shop near Hythe,
Myra now appeared as acting lookout for Marcus or the
Major or both, with or without the knowledge of either:
Myra perpetually on the spot and watchful, in all the
unhopeful prospect, for the hopeful event that might
force the guardian of the treasure into surrendering all
or part of it.

And Myra, eavesdropping, had ferreted out the event:
the cruel pinch that threatened an extremely aged
woman with the loss of her home. Leaving Mowbray's
would be death to her, in the literal sense; Ground between the millstones of this prospect and her resolve to
keep the letters intact, she must sacrifice the resolve. . . .
To whom would Myra run first with the glad news of
the vulnerable moment? To Grant, or Marcus? Marcus
sounded the better pay. Or was she negotiating with the
two of them, playing both ends against the middle . . . ?

And now that she had split her head in clarifying this much of it she should be at rest, her dissatisfactions allayed. . . . They were not allayed; a chafing residue was left in her, a sense of some important omission, if only she could force it from depletion. . . . A headache was all she had gained so far from racking her brains on Champernowne's time. She must escape into the fresh air if only for a moment, and thoroughly out of humour put on her coat and hat. And again, by untiring paradox, it was the sight of Tim at the end of a corridor that gave her the answer, and its shaming obviousness the force that pushed her out of the library as fast as she could go, and into the nearest call-box.

'John,' she appealed, having found him at his London flat that was also his office; as an art consultant his knowledge of dealers big and small, legitimate and illegitimate, English, American and European, was encyclopaedic. 'John, would you know of a dealer—or maybe just an expert in old documents—named Marcus?'

'No,' he returned after the briefest pause. 'I don't.'

'You're sure?' she persisted. 'He gave me the feeling he was in—in rather an active way of business.'

'Old documents,' he ruminated. 'English, was he? American?'

'Naturalized English, I expect—speaks with an accent.'

'No, I've never run across him. What does he look like?'

'Well, he's small and bald and—and rather globular. Very pleasant and polite, but rather oily. And well-dressed, very smart and—' she ransacked her memory '—wears a rimless pince-nez with a thin gold chain attached to his lapel.'

'Braun,' came the answer at once. He spelled it. 'Accent, you said? bald, fat, ingratiating? pince-nez on a chain? Sounds like Braun.'

'I see,' she returned, nonplussed again. 'Well, thank you very much, John.'

'You're welcome. And by the way, who told you documents?'

'Doesn't he—?'

'Not that I ever heard of. Stamps, dear girl, nothing but stamps. And if anyone you know is doing business with him,' he concluded, 'tell them to keep their eyes well and truly peeled.'

She went out and walked, bemused, thinking of Tim and his guess; she gave him full marks, clever boy. Letters of that period might be infinitely less valuable than the stamps they carried, stamps of earliest issues, scarcities and possibly rarities. . . .

With cataleptic suddenness she halted in her tracks as a new theory powerfully ousted an old one. Rather than that Myra had met this Braun through the offices of Major Grant, how much more likely it was—how excitingly more likely—that Braun was the one who had bought the first fruits of her pilferings from the library; she the thief, he the receiver. Now, with appetite whetted by this first taste of blood, with his nose for profit quickened by Myra's nearness to a rumoured hoard, he had come down himself to smell out the lay of the land. Nor had his effort been wasted, any more than his withdrawal was a sign of failure. Dealers were used to long and patient manoeuvres, to repeated and devious approaches. If the present hour were unpropitious, he had left a spy in the camp to inform him of an hour more favourable. . . .

By now he would have been told that the old woman was threatened with actual homelessness. No immediate threat, the compassionate Caroline would stave it off as long as possible, but it must loom nearer and nearer, inexorably. Then, probably, the next manifestation: the reappearance of Marcus on the scene. . . . And none of all this might be true, she reminded herself, it was nothing but guesswork and invention à la Tim. Yet how it cleared up certain obscurities, how naturally it all hung together. . . .

Turning to go back, she found herself concentrating equally on a sort of mental debit and credit, two columns side by side. In one was her secret possession of certain facts; in the other, Myra's version of the self-same facts. She had denied acquaintance with Marcus; she had connived at his alias; she had given a false account of Caroline's acceptance of him; when cornered by the meeting at the George and Crown she had given a doctored version of his business as well as (very likely) a fictitious account of their manner of first acquaintance. Totting up and comparing the various items made it hard, in fact, to escape the conclusion that Myra—in addition to her strange new inequalities of character since college days—had become a thorough-paced liar.

XI

As it happened, the penitential dinner in her chapter of amends encountered an unforeseen setback. Mrs. Lees-Milburn caught a heavy cold lasting the better part of a month; with the disappearance of the cold she found, to her indescribable rage, that she had completely lost her sense of taste.

'No use your wining and dining me when I can't tell meet from cheese,' she gritted resentfully. 'When I eat expensive food, I want to *taste* it. I'll let you know when I'm all right again.'

Also as it happened, it could not be anticipated—least of all by Alison—how considerable a misfortune this postponement should turn out to be, how dire a captivity. She was near to completing, fom the chaos of the Tollemache papers, a first rough classification. This was a good and permissible jumping-off place if she wanted to use it as such; a strategic moment for resigning, if she still wanted to resign. And her present need to resign, radically different from her first need, was owing to her own fatal assumption that she had mastered the emotion he roused in her. His wife's allusion to his hidden affair, plus her own self-exhortation, had broken the force of his attraction for her—she thought. Then to her horror she felt it surging back regardless; the longing to see him, the starving need for the few daily moments in his presence. And instead of saving herself by the one means in her power, a dignified withdrawal, she found herself inventing pretexts to linger. She must wait till Mrs. Lees-Milburn was well, too cruel to cheat the old woman of her little festivity, so looked-forward-to and so infrequent. . . . In a last despairing effort she recalled his frequent absences overnight. Not all for a sick father, not all by any means. . . . Her pride, fiercely invoked, responded with not even a twitch. *I don't care*, she thought abandonedly. *He's sleeping with someone else and I'm in love with him.* Her abject servitude she would drag back with her to London, the lengthening chain with a vengeance, and wait till time rusted it off her.

In this parching waste where she strayed by her own choice, one event reared up sharply; a person walking toward her in the street one day, and herself walking toward the person. This time no one was at her elbow to nudge her and say, *See that woman?* and she needed no one; by instinct, she knew. Strikingly elegant even in distant silhouette, the stranger was an actual exotic on these old worn flagstones, perambulated mostly by retired gentlefolk in substantial woollens. At closer range her other aspects revealed themselves—a haughty aquiline face, an aura of devouring egotism; her very step—elongated, feline, eating up distance with effortless grace —was predatory. She half-glanced at Alison in passing, and the single un-look marked the automatic hater of all women and the vicious hater of young women—all the more vicious for being, herself, a bit long in the tooth.

So, she thought, moving more slowly; so this was what he was up against. Her poor love with his innate fineness, gentleness, chivalry; an unequal match for this indecent personified greed. Had it been at the library today, the walking greed? was it going there later? Its mere presence in the neighbourhood must mean one or the other.

. . . Alison, presumably a civilized woman, let her mind dwell yearningly on the pleasure of raking that face with her nails, one good, soul-satisfying rip. . . .

With a sigh she roused herself from her access of championship; offspring of useless love and professional friendship. *Mild* professional friendship, she qualified again, and sighed again. Just as well to restrain her protective fervour for a man who neither wanted her love, nor needed her protection.

Mrs. Lees-Milburn, recovering, was not backward in reminding Alison of their postponed engagement. In consequence, on this Saturday night, they sat facing each other across a small table in the restaurant of Folkestone's best hotel. The big room was not crowded but surprisingly full for the time of year; lights shone, waiters were brisk, smells of good cooking suggested themselves in well-bred diminuendo, and a string trio on a dais sugared the air with harmless concords and rhythms. The weather was bad, in fact prohibitive, but apparently it required an actual convulsion of nature to inhibit the national passion for weekends.

To this glittering occasion Mrs. Lees-Milburn had done honour in a grisly getup straight from a waxworks museum, a sweeping dress of black crepe darkly criss-crossed with tarnished gold thread, and with a wide black satin bib let into its front. Within the confines of this bib, overlapping them here and there, she had pinned without rhyme or reason a mass of trinkets that made her hostess blink as they caught the overhead lights—yet all of it, as Myra had said, decidedly of lesser grade; ugly brooches set with small dingy stones, two watches in green enamel and rose enamel respectively and neither of them working, Alison would guess, for many years.

If I ate like that I'd be dead, she thought with admiration and envy, and certainly the old woman's performance was awe-inspiring. A couple of stiff martinis to begin, a big plate of thick oyster soup (the hotel still did some old-fashioned cooking), a token serving of turbot with lobster sauce but a far-from-token entrée of veal done with cheese and ham and generously *garni;* along with this she had accounted for most of a bottle of Montrachet chosen by herself, having imperiously scouted the sommelier's suggestion of 'a nice carafe' and sent him away a broken man. As single-mindedly as a child she sat luxuriating in the brightness, the animation, the food and wine—a mood which her companion had begun to observe no less single-mindedly, if from motives no longer creditable.

In truth, her original purity of thanksgiving—the expensive ordeal of a whole evening with Mrs. Lees-Milburn, in return for still having Chris—began to be tarnished with calculation. If she were in for the joyless assignment of companioning this grotesque in public, she might as well get something out of it. The old woman was an inexhaustible source of local information, past and present; if anyone knew the identity of Durant's concealed mistress, she would. Let her be warmed up first, well lubricated, then entice her gently into the subject . . . disgusting tactics, she was a jackal prowling compulsively about the carrion of her own torment, but her curiosity had become a worse torment, raging. . . . She began keeping watch, spying ignobly—behind her irreproachable smile and manner—for the climax of overfeeding and its accompaniment of loquacity, more unrestrained than usual. . . . .

And the moment had arrived now, perhaps, in a lull between musical selections; the cessation of strings and piano made a sudden silence in the room, almost a hush. In company with this hush Mrs. Lees-Milburn laid down her knife and fork with an air of work well done.

'Very good,' she pronounced. 'Very good indeed.' Spiritually she was licking her chops. 'Very nice music too, nice and loud.' The absence of harmonic background seemed to reach her belatedly. 'Why aren't they playing?'

'They will in a moment.' Wishing in aside that the old woman would keep her voice down—it seemed more shattering this evening than usual—she made a trial cast. 'Mrs. Lees-Milburn, don't you ever use the library? I don't believe I've ever seen you in the reading-room.'

'How's that?'

Alison began repeating, and was cut off by a strident, '*Read?* goodness no. Too busy living in my day to do much reading. Can't acquire the habit now—too late, I expect.' Her tone was unregretful. 'Never did it, so don't miss it.—Does Tom Durant work you very hard?'

'Oh no, not hard.' The sweet sickening qualm all through her, at the name, was offset by satisfaction; the old woman had taken the bait.

'D'you like him?' the ancient was demanding.

'Yes, he's quite pleasant to work for,' she returned judicially. 'Very considerate.'

'How's that?'

Alison's repetition, this time, was conditioned by a new awareness: that Mrs. Lees-Milburn, in the wake of her cold, had grown considerably deaf; her inability to gauge the volume of her own voice was another sign of it.

'His father's at a nursing home in Hythe,' the old woman pursued, promisingly. 'I believe I've told you that he was very ill—?'

'Yes.'

'He won't last much longer now, old Michael Durant.

Charming man, delightful, widower for donkey's years—
he and Tom always very close. When he dies,' she fixed
Alison with a significant eye, 'Tom will be rather well-off.
Not wealthy, but quite well-off.'

'Oh?'

'He's hard-up at the moment, of course. That leech he
married takes his last penny, or good as—but when Michael goes, he'll be all right. That house of theirs—' she
interrupted herself for a healthy swig of wine, rolling it
in her mouth with eyes half-closed and a look of concentration. 'Very decent wine this, nice bouquet.—Where
was I?'

'The house, Mr. Durant's—'

'Oh yes. Well, as I was saying, even if the tax-vultures
take the last of the money, there's that big old house of
theirs, huge garden—get an absolute fortune for it. What's
Tom want with it, one man alone?'

'He could live there,' she suggested ingenuously. 'He's
married.'

'Married!' Mrs. Lees-Milburn bristled. 'You've been
here all this time, and don't know they've separated?'

'Separated couples sometimes make it up.'

'He and that harpy? have you ever *seen* her?'

'No,' she lied.

'That accounts for it. The woman's vile, that's all, a
nasty, promiscuous . . . a wonder that some of the lot
she runs with wouldn't do for her, one of these days.'

A chill touched her strangely, a qualm of knowledge
and premonition: *But then he'll be suspected, the husband always is first of all, and what if he can't clear himself?* Her moment of fear ebbed; listening again to the
character-assassination flowing on unchecked, she as-
sessed her progress and was inclined to be pleased with
it so far. Now it only remained to watch her chance, in-

sinuate one or two more leading questions . . . the vilifi-
cation seemed to run down; she flung herself upon the
lull.

'But Mrs. Lees-Milburn, Mr. Durant might want his
house later, mightn't he?' she fished with shameless in-
nocence. 'Men do marry again, you know,' and held her
breath.

'Marry again—?'

Into this moment, so painfully achieved, the dessert
trolley chose to come rolling up alongside. At once Mrs.
Lees-Milburn transferred her whole attention and bent
on the display a long and analytical gaze. When a mon-
strous helping of trifle drowned in a suave lake of cream
was before her she picked up her fork and spoon, delaying
only long enough to look disparagingly at Alison's orange
in curaçao and ask, 'D'you really *like* that?'

'Well, I've eaten such a lot.' The excuse concealed the
raging frustration of a tigress. Just as she had got the
oracle nicely warmed-up and moving in the right direction, the beastly trolley had had to crash in with its load
of beastly sugar, so that beastly people already gorged
could gorge themselves still further. Fatal derailment,
and how get it back on the track again while the old
woman sat absorbed in her pudding, while her spoon
rose and fell in relentless rhythm . . . when the Chinese
nobility on the plates began to appear through the shal-
lows of cream she threw herself into a solitary, last-ditch
effort: 'Don't they?'

'How's that?'

'Men.' The noisy room covered her trumpeting voice.
'They do marry again, so mightn't Mr. Durant?'

'Tom Durant marry again?' The mere tone of the question was a death-knell. 'I'd say he's got enough on his
plate without, for the moment. Let him peel off this leech

first, before he takes on another . . .' Her voice had begun straying, in consonance with her straying attention.

'From what one hears,' Alison shouted despairingly,
'men separated from their wives usually have the next
candidate in view, before they divorce.'

'Maybe.' She was not being discreet, she had only lost
interest. 'Nowadays anything's possible.' Her mind was
running ahead on coffee and brandy, her restive eyes
counted the people already leaving the restaurant. 'See,
they're all going to the ballroom. We'd better look smart,
m'dear, or we shan't get a table.' With decision she
jettisoned her napkin and rose, while Alison hastily dug
out a tip and scrambled after.

Their sojourn in the ballroom was the sojourn of all
non-dancers. The big room brayed deafeningly with the
frenetic beat of the dance-band; the floor thundered and
shook with the combined assaults upon it. The elders one-
stepped or waltzed gracefully and skilfully, and the
young somehow made nonsense of this grace and skill
as they stomped, writhed and twisted in violent con-
frontations which must end then and there—apparently—
in rape or murder on the ballroom floor.

'Why don't they dislocate something?' the old lady
asked once, with evident wishfulness and disappointment. Through a dense fog of cigarette-smoke their
coffee had found them with comforting promptness; Mrs.
Lees-Milburn, having had one brandy, signified her desire for a second.

'That was nice, very nice,' murmured the old woman.
'Thank you very much, m'dear.' Her voice was drowsy
and sated; she belched voluptuously. 'We might do this
again, one evening before you leave.' She appeared to

go to sleep but continued sitting upright, her head nodding and jerking to the rhythm of the taxi.

Meanwhile Alison could confront, wryly, the expensive evening that had turned up zero. As against the failure of her shameful pumping attempt, however, she could set one definite gain: that if even Mrs. Lees-Milburn knew nothing of Tom Durant's clandestine affair, no one knew. How preciously he was guarding his love, the woman he was going to marry. . . .

'Ow,' she said involuntarily; the bright painful stab of jealousy within her had coincided with the taxi's halt.

'We're there,' she announced.

'How's . . . that . . . ?'

'We're home.' The taxi stank of drink at second-hand; little of this aroma, she felt, was her contribution. 'Let me help you.' She got out, wondering how to manoeuvre this tall tiddly bulk into the house and up to her room. She had not reckoned, however, with Mrs. Lees-Milburn's power of resurrection. The old woman roused galvanically, lurched from the seat and down to the pavement, ignoring the outstretched hand; Alison, stopping to pay, glanced apprehensively after her and saw her making good time up the front steps, swaying hardly at all. As they passed into the hall it was obvious that she was wide-awake again and quite steady, and once more Alison paid a lesser mortal's tribute to a constitution of granite, indestructible. They went upstairs together, punctiliously putting out lights, and after good-nights and renewed thanks, separated.

In her room, she saw with surprise that it was only eleven; time had seemed to stretch on and on. Only eleven, yet within these walls it felt late, profoundly late; the house silent as the grave, everyone asleep. Feeling cross and cheated she started to undress, then with astonishment heard the noise at her door—the furtive hurried tapping, repeated and repeated. The sound immobilized her for only an instant; she was in a good frame of mind to deal with Myra. Whipping on her dressing-gown she advanced grimly and flung the door open—not on Myra, but on her guest of the evening.

Taken aback in unison, in unison they began to apologize; the old woman's strident whisper overbore Alison's.

'Sorry, sorry,' she hissed. 'But someone's been in my room tonight.' No fear was perceptible in her, only fury. 'While we were out.'

Nonplussed, the other stood for a moment before managing uncertainly, 'You're sure—?'

'Come and see.' It was less invitation than command; obediently Alison followed, tying the cord of her robe. As easily as that, as simply, she passed into the holy of holies that Myra would have given a couple of teeth to enter. The ironic thought yielded, by help of a dim night-light, to an impression of familiarity; of old women ending their days in hotels and guest-houses, this was not the first such room she had seen. Small rooms or medium rooms crammed with mastodon pieces bought for big spacious houses; pieces specially cherished, sometimes fine and valuable but sometimes—as now—merely tasteless, elaborate and cumbersome, and costly in their day. There loomed darkly the old woman's double four-poster with suffocating brocade curtains; a huge mahogany secretary; a deep leather armchair and a clutter of china odds and ends on small tables. There also, pushed against the foot of the bed, stood a rectangular mass dissimulated by a cover of stiff tapestry whose left-hand edge, crookedly displaced, revealed. . . .

'You see!' sibilated Mrs. Lees-Milburn, pointing dramatically. 'I *know* that cover wasn't awry like that, when I left!'

With unqualified blankness Alison regarded the big old-fashioned trunk, of the kind that had guaranteed rupture to generations of porters. Approaching, she could see better what concealed it—a piece of gros-point re-embroidered with silk, faded now and ragged; its up-turned corner disclosed its canvas backing.

'Could we have more light?' she ventured.

'Eh?'

'A little more light,' Alison raised her voice, 'or we can't see anything.'

Mrs. Lees-Milburn turned on an overhead light of low wattage, after which the visitant evolved perforce a first question, 'Is anything missing?'

'Missing—?'

'Jewellery, money, anything—?'

'I haven't looked.'

'Then how do you know—'

'I'd all my jewellery on this evening,' the old woman interrupted, 'and I don't keep *large* sums of money in my room.' Giving Alison no time to admire the majesty of this implication, she swept on, 'This, this!' and pointed. '*This* is what they're after, all of them!'

Alison hesitated again, thinking hard but not very profitably. She stood on the threshold of a temple called monomania, its dusty altar served by one dusty old priestess; every word of hers from now on must be judged with care.

'Perhaps—' she was speaking much more loudly than she liked, to make the old woman hear '—if you'd take the cover off—?'

Mrs. Lees-Milburn swept the tapestry aside, and Alison knelt down and looked at the old-fashioned brass lock, probably standard in its day. So far as she could see there was absolutely no sign that force had been used; still, by describing the trunk in any luggage shop, it seemed all too easy that a key might be obtained. . . .

'I don't see scratches, or anything like that,' she said, getting up. 'Perhaps later on you can see if anything's been taken out.'

As she moved tactfully toward the door the old woman was rooting somewhere; a ring of keys clattered.

'Don't go!' commanded Mrs. Lees-Milburn. 'Don't go!' As her guest halted in astonishment she was turning the key with manifest ease—proving at least that the lock had neither been forced nor jammed—flung up the lid and lifted out a layer of crushed and tattered wadding, identifiable as a once-splendid Indian shawl with the rare cream-coloured centre. Advancing to stand beside her, bemused with surprise and unreality, Alison regarded row upon row of faded envelopes and faded writing; all in small bundles tied with dim ribbons, with the tight brittle look of having lain undisturbed for years. Here in this secret and unworked lode who knew what re-creation of Victoria's reign might exist; that reign so thronged with great and near-great names that dozens rose at the most casual summons. From Dickens to Carlyle, from Arnold to Jowett, then the more solitary comets, Disraeli, Nightingale. . . .

'Does it look as though it'd been touched?' she asked finally.

'Well—no.' The old woman was reluctant. 'It seems to be in order.'

'I'd say so too. I only—' she voiced her first misgiving from the moment the trunk-lid was lifted '—I only hope there's nothing in them.'

'How's that?'

'I hope they're not infested,' she explained loudly, 'with parasites, paper-mites—anything that eats paper.'

'Mercy!' The priestess of the cult was palpably startled. 'I'd never thought of that, never!'

'At any rate, I don't believe anyone's been in here.' Suddenly tired of the whole alcoholic performance, she wanted only to escape. 'It certainly doesn't look that way.'

'The cover,' insisted Mrs. Lees-Milburn. 'I *know* it was on straight when I left.'

'But it's very stiff,' Alison argued less patiently. 'You might easily brush against it and not know. I don't believe anyone's been in here, Mrs. Lees-Milburn—I shouldn't worry if I were you.'

'Well . . .' beginning dubiously, all at once the old woman changed course. 'What you said about insects in my collection, it's fearfully worrying. Would you, m'dear,' she appealed, 'look them over for me one day soon, see if there's been any damage—?'

'Yes indeed,' Alison returned numbly, after a pause of unbelief. 'If you like.'

'There're very few people I'd trust, but I trust you. I only hope,' lamented the ancient, trailing Alison to the door, 'they're not chewed to bits, by this time—?'

'I don't expect so,' she soothed, over an unforeseen pang; with sudden compassion she saw Mrs. Lees-Milburn as a poor worried old thing in need of help, solitary in having outlived her generation, defenceless and disliked. 'There'd be signs of it,' she continued to reassure. 'Discolouration and crumbling and a rather strong smell. I expect they're all right, Mrs. Lees-Milburn, they're quite all right.'

'Soon, you must look at them soon. And thank you, m'dear, thank you very much, so sorry to bother you—'

Thankful to hear the door close on profuse gratitude, she was not instantly aware of the shadowed recess of a doorway nor of the figure standing silent and motionless within it.

Her involuntary start was simultaneous with the figure's putting itself in motion and approaching swiftly.

'You sneak,' Myra hissed at her. 'You sly contemptible sneak.' Between the schoolgirl abuse and the adult venom that powered it was a bitterly laughable incongruity. 'I knew it, all along I've known—!' As mere astonishment held the other wordless, she gestured imperiously. 'My room and be quick, you'd better. Or yours.'

'No,' said Alison, recovering. 'Not in my room and not in yours. Good-night.'

'Don't try that on, don't *dare!*' Myra's hand, shooting out with manifest purpose, checked nevertheless within a quarter-inch of Alison's arm and hovered there, shaking.

'You'd better not touch me,' murmured the object of surveillance, pleasantly.

'So you've got the inside track, have you.' Myra let her arm fall. '*You've* no interest in that trunk of hers! *You've* no axe of your own to grind. Oh no! Liar! you beastly liar!'

'I've no interest in the trunk and no axe to grind,' Alison said briefly. 'Good heavens, this perpetual spying of yours—it's intolerable.'

'Sucking up to that mouldy old scarecrow, dining and wining her—for the pleasure of it?' Myra accused from between clenched teeth. 'Don't make me laugh.'

'Better not let her find you out here, she's just in the mood to start a brawl.' Alison began turning away. 'She'll be coming out to the bathroom any moment now.'

'Let her,' invited Myra, all the same casting an uneasy

glance at the old woman's door. 'What were you doing in her room?'

'None of your affair.'

'She's never let *any*one in there, in all the years I've been here, only Caroline and the cleaner. And after a couple of months, barely, she lets *you* in!' Myra's head thrust forward, a viperine gesture. 'I heard you all right, the way you had to yell at her, deaf old besom—!'

'Ear to the door?' Alison murmured. 'Again?'

'She unlocked the trunk,' Myra panted, oblivious of insult. 'I heard the click, I heard the lid being raised, then you—you—you said something about papers, the condition—you did, you did—!'

Once more Alison stood wordless, not from unreadiness this time and not from fear; her power of simply walking away checked by the mere grotesqueness of the scene. The semi-darkness, the palpitating hatred in the air, the exchange of abrasive whispers, above all the figure swathed in its dun-coloured robe; Myra in the grip of some transport that changed her to something baleful, hardly recognizable. All of it unreal and hypnotic, like those dreams where one stands paralyzed in the face of some oncoming disaster . . .

'Listen to me, Myra.' With an effort she broke free of the spell, her low voice checking the other visibly. 'Don't mention this again, don't talk to me about it ever again, do you hear?' She drew an audible breath. 'Or don't talk to me at all. Not about anything—I'd like that just as well.'

The feeling of sanctuary when she gained her room drained out of her and was followed by a weakness that, to her own surprise, sat her down abruptly on the edge of the bed. Nothing really, she thought, leaning forward with her head in her hands; a nasty little quarrel, nothing really, but the impact of it was catching up disagreeably. . . .

And catching up only now, with belated unwelcome clairvoyance she saw Myra; not this or that aspect of Myra but all of Myra, in the round. Not only Myra greedy and hopeless, craning her neck at Mrs. Lees-Milburn's grapes, but Myra padding like a dangerous animal up and down a narrow cage; trapped by her ill-paid job, by the quiet village, by the social monotony. The change in her for the worse Alison now saw as a mounting desperation, a struggle to break out of the cage before it was too late—and then a bleaker thought: their old friendship, holding by fewer and fewer threads since her first arrival, and the last of these threads just now frayed apart, broken past repair. Sad all of it, disheartening and sad. . . .

She resumed undressing, every now and again murmuring *Oh dear*, a sighing uninflected lament, *Oh dear*. In bed her pervasive melancholy changed to vague drifts of thought, good for nothing but to spoil sleep. Someone in the old woman's room? her imagination plus a slight tipsiness? Or perhaps not? Then her growing deafness, Myra by the way had noticed it too. . . . Above all, her sensational offer to let the correspondence be examined: had she meant it actually, or was it another random shoot of Montrachet and two cognacs? Well, she would either forget about it or refer to it sometime; perhaps even tomorrow, tomorrow was Sunday. . . .

The thought of Sunday inspired her with sudden abhorrence; she began casting about for escape. Run away, as she had done before? Run to London, to the empty flat, the empty day, since she had made no arrangement with friends? No good, think quickly of her pole star, think of Chris. . . . she stared aghast, wide-eyed in the dark, at the new shipwreck that confronted her. For the first time in her life the thought of her son, that could disperse her utmost loneliness, left her as lonely as before. Still incredulous at the failure of this unfailing light—*Another light*, she thought incredibly. *Something beside Chris, something else. Or no,* she reaffirmed her treachery, *not something else, someone else,* and made a curious sound in the darkness, not a laugh and not a sob.

All at once the pattern of her life rose before her in the shape of library workrooms and search-rooms, all more or less identical; hollow cells in the chain of cells where she—a patient drudge—walked the treadmill of respectable literate labour.

A wildness rose in her, as wildly fought; this sudden bankruptcy must end in crying. She had not cried for years, the thought of crying was panic, a trembling panic she must succumb to, cry and cry her heart out. . . .

This disintegration she was able to control, but not the image that had given it birth: the bone-white cube awaiting her on Monday and on all days, the empty husk in which she rattled around forever, with herself and her whole life drying up.

XII

The words shattered on her ear with incomprehensible distinctness, honed to a sharper edge by the bare work-room. Startled, her hands arrested, she raised her head and stared first with astonishment, then with horror at the door—sagging open by no more than a hair's-breadth, yet its angle within the door-frame was perceptible if one looked. Failure of the latch to engage, a thing unknown with this heavy door and its superlative fittings of an earlier day. Once more her remote awareness of talk next door had been muted by her obliviousness, but there was no ignoring the pitch of this present voice, by no means unknown to her.

'How dare you!' it screeched on a sudden high note. 'I won't!'

'You will,' said the husband of Esmé Durant.

'No! I won't take it!'

'You'll take that, or nothing.'

'Why, you—you miserable, cheap, cheating . . .'

A double consideration halted the eavesdropper's sudden rising and first urgent step forward: her exact picture of the office and its dispositions. Durant was sitting at the desk with his back squarely toward the door and his wife, across from him, was as squarely facing it. Its most imperceptible closing movement might catch her eye, that vulturine eye that missed nothing; the click of the engaging latch might also be beyond prevention. Even so, nothing worse could happen but an invasion of her room, unpleasantly vituperative no doubt but not all that alarming. . . .

This minor misgiving, however, withered and disappeared before her actual fear for the man next door, sitting out abuse and invective as he had always done, with patience and self-control. Yet this time—

This is the one too many, she thought, suddenly cold with premonition. *This time she's gone too far, something's going to happen. Now, now, any moment now.* With absolute certainty of instinct she felt him being pushed beyond the limits of endurance to the point where something must break, the Fourth Man must take over, and in agonies of apprehension waited for the portents: his chair scraped back suddenly and savagely, sounds of terror punctuated with violence, blows heavy or even lethal. And no one could blame him, the provocation had been repeated and unbearable, yet no argument on earth could prevent his life from lying in ruins from that moment. . . .

'Be quiet,' Durant's voice pierced through her tension of waiting. 'And listen—'

'No!'

'Another word from you and I'll put you out of the place bodily, myself.'

The assurance in his voice, even a sort of placidity, locked the hearer this time into a different paralysis—astonishment.

'Good!' his wife was jeering hatefully. 'Good for your holy image.'

'Not good for mine but not for yours either,' he returned. 'And I'll see to that, I'll make it my business. Listen now, you'd better.'

On the heels of her reprieve from one fear, came consternation at another. He was about to speak of intimate and private arrangements and there was no way she could warn him that none of it was, in fact, intimate nor private. His voice, not at all raised, had force and weight; without listening, she had to hear. Frantically she longed to contract, disappear into any hole; he would never forgive her for overhearing if he found out, and there was every chance he would find out. . . .

'I couldn't talk earlier,' he was saying, 'because of Father, the uncertainty . . . but there's no more uncertainty.'

He paused as if daring her to cheer at the news; her silence was—apparently—prudent refusal of the dare.

'Don't think I'm anticipating his death—' the subtlest change shadowed his voice on *death* '—but I've got to anticipate certain conditions afterward. Now listen,' he repeated. 'Everything I'm going to say rests on your beginning an action for divorce, straightaway. On that condition.' He paused. 'On that one, single condition.'

Silence, absolute yet watchful.

'We've been apart for nearly three years,' he pursued. 'By the time you petition, it will be three years. Now I want you to go to Bradley, who will draw up an agreement valid only—*only*,' he repeated, 'in case the divorce is final. And if it is—' he paused again '—whatever I get from the sale of the house, you're guaranteed twelve thousand pounds out of it.'

'No!' she protested with fury. 'You promised me all of it—!'

'So I did, like a fool,' he said imperturbably. 'That was when I was willing to lie down and let you pick me clean. Now I'm not willing, that's all.'

'Ah.' She laughed savagely. 'You sound as if you've been finding out the value of the house.'

'I have done,' he agreed. 'Why not?'

'And if you suppose,' she pursued with mounting fury, 'you'll fob me off with a lousy twelve thousand pounds, think again. You and Bradley, thinking you'll crowd me into a divorce on your terms, not mine! This agreement you're proposing—anything signed under coercion or bribery's no good, you fool, even I know that much. Of all the bloody neck, saying I'll get the money if I divorce you—!'

'Not if,' he corrected mildly. 'Not *if* we're divorced, only in case. You get it *in case* we're divorced.'

'You think you'll get around it with a dirty little trick of words, you and your slimy solicitor,' she shouted. 'Well, you know what you can do with your agreement.'

'You won't sign it?'

'*No!*'

'Very good, you won't.'

His tone was a sort of shock; Alison, once more bracing herself against some violence of outrage, was unprepared for this flawless equanimity.

'In that case,' he was saying, 'let's review the position. You're living now on what I give you, while waiting for my father's death to better my position financially. Well, don't base your hopes on that any longer. The money's more or less gone—the nursing-home, operations and so forth—and after death duties I don't expect a penny. There'll be nothing left, but the house.'

'Valuable,' she mocked, 'when you sell it.'

'Valuable,' he returned, '*if* I sell it. And rather than let you profit by the sale, I'll let it drop to pieces first—make up your mind to that. But I shan't let it drop to pieces either,' he assured her. 'I'll live in it, however it's run-down. No power on earth can make me sell, if I don't want to sell.'

Even a room away, the gathering stillness was explosive.

'You promised me the house,' stifled accents broke it. 'The *whole* house, the *whole* price for it, you nasty slippery—'

'Or if we don't divorce,' he interrupted, still with that imperturbable calm, 'let's review your own position. You're living now on what I give you, and it's not the style you care for if I know anything about it. Meanwhile your grip on Basil, or available replacements, keeps slipping. If a kindly providence makes you a widow, I gave up my insurances a couple of years ago, and I'll arrange that you get nothing from the house. Or suppose—' he had ignored the very curious sound she made '—you begin proceedings at once for increased maintenance, on the grounds that I've lied to you about my resources. Well, I shouldn't advise it. First I'm not lying, and second you might get an unsympathetic divorce judge—the kind who doesn't see why an able-bodied woman, fairly young, shouldn't earn at least part of her living.'

Another loaded pause followed.

'So don't sneeze at my offer, it's by far your best bet. If you be not fair for Basil with twelve thousand pounds . . .' His mockery died almost before it was born. 'That much I promise you definitely. By all the signs it'll be a quick sale, so quick money for you.' Another pause. '*If* we're divorced.'

'All right,' a sullen voice came, after a thick interval. 'All right, you rotten cut-throat, I'll go to your Bradley.'

'At once.'

'Yes, yes, at once.'

It was over, thought the victim of the defaulting latch, thank God it was over. The woman would leave now, he would be going to lunch directly after and perhaps without noticing the door. . . . Instead of sounds of departure, however, there struck on her astounded ear something quite different.

'What's happened to you?' demanded Esmé Durant.

'Nothing,' he said politely. 'That I know of.'

'You're different,' she insisted. Her tone, suddenly altered, was speculative and curious—an uneasy blend. 'Something . . . something's made you different.'

'Has it?' he returned with total indifference.

'Yes. You weren't—you weren't like this, ever before. —Is it your girl-friend?' she jeered cautiously. 'Has she been talking some guts into you?'

'If you like.' His impassivity was always more excluding.

'No, but really,' she persisted. 'You've changed all at once, you're . . . tough. I always liked a tough man.' Her voice, transparent betrayer of her every inward strategy, slithered into furtive propitiation, even flattery. 'If you'd been a bit tougher with me—kept a harder hand on me—everything might have been different.' With a wary flirtatiousness, with ignominious blandishment, she slid another degree toward the approaches of reconciliation. 'Even now, maybe it isn't too—'

'For God's sake.' His amiable contempt was so devastating that even the invisible hearer winced. She could follow likewise, and with intimate understanding, the ensuing pause: the pause needed by a coarse and conceited woman to realize that she had lost a man for good.

'I don't think I like this a whole lot,' announced Esmé Durant. With ludicrous speed her voice had taken on an ugliness as yet restrained by calculation. 'There must be *some* dodge in this sudden change of yours—some dirty little reason.'

'No reason. Or shall we say—' his tone, indestructibly

polite, held a weariness '—that I've once seen Shelley plain?'

'What?'

'Or swap Esmé for Shelley, and let it go at that?'

'All right, you swine!' she shrieked; by the sound, she had jumped up. 'All right, damn your soul, I'll go to Bradley. This is n-nothing but sharp p-practise—black-mail—' she fought for breath '—and you *know* it!'

The office door slammed shatteringly.

With the violent relief that almost escaped her in audible exhalation—that she caught back just in time—ran an echoing puzzlement to Esmé Durant's, followed by comprehension hardly welcome, to say the least of it. The two embroilments she had been forced to overhear; his behaviour the first time and the second, as if two different men were involved; the first one spinelessly sub-mitting to extortion, the second hard as nails, without effort bringing the extortioner to heel. . . . For a change so radical, as even that coarse stupid woman had guessed, there must be a powerful reason, and her guess as to its nature had been—in all likelihood—completely right. But anyone could guess, there was little mystery about what was so exactly her own case. Having some-one to love, protect and fight for, armed you immeasur-ably; he had been re-armed, by what secret exchanges between him and another woman, only themselves knew. Just as she had Chris to strengthen her, so he had his cherished secret love. . . .

Abruptly stifling the thought, she returned to the prob-abilities of the next few moments. He must be leaving at once, or soon; give him a good start, then bolt out her-self and find a pot of tea in a healing solitude. . . . No sound came from next door, no movement. He was taking a moment to recover, he needed it worse than she did. Strange if he did not, she thought on an inward sigh, and sat waiting patiently and confidently till she heard the outer door close.

The sight of her own door opening instead—the last thing she expected—transfixed her with incredulity, then horror; as the aperture widened unhurriedly and admitted him, she started up with exactly the look of a thief caught in the act.

'I—I wanted to close it,' she blurted. 'But I was afraid it'd be heard—or noticed—'

He said something, inaudible beneath her tumbling disjointed apology.

'—I couldn't help hearing, I'm sorry, so—'

'I left the door open myself,' he repeated calmly. 'I wanted you to hear.'

An apartness took her, the vacant moment called fugue. The flash had been too blinding to interpret; in this vacuum, without belief and without hope, she opposed his unmistakable meaning with her long dedication to bad luck, her settled and passive belief that happiness was not for her. And the approach of happiness, mysteriously incarnate in the approaching man, roused in her nothing but distrust and readiness for flight as she stood perfectly still, watching him like a cornered animal. The grasp of his arms, not gentle, turned her with shaming rapidity into something unrecognizable; in the scholarly room they kissed in a fashion by no means scholarly, kissed and kissed with the fury of starvation under the cold neon brightness, the chill silence . . .

She began struggling against him with panic so genuine that he released her partly, then entirely, with an astonishment as manifest as her violence.

'I'm—I'm sorry,' she gabbled, and brushed pathetically

at her disordered hair. 'But I don't—I don't—' Forcibly she took herself in hand; he was staring blankly, and she had to explain. 'All I want is to be with you, it's all I want—'

'Well?' he interrupted harshly.

'—but—but—a short affair, no. You've every right to amuse yourself, but—'

'What the devil are you talking about?'

'—but for me, a—an interim affair,' she floundered wildly, making a worse and worse mess of it, 'and then to lose you—no, I don't think I could bear it. Don't be angry,' she implored. 'But I mean, since you've someone you're going to marry—'

'Where did you get that idea?' he cut her off abrasively.

'From—in your office—that first time.' She gestured. 'She was yelling so I couldn't help—I mean—she said that you'd someone but she didn't know whom. She said it more than once, she—she kept on and on about it.'

'I see,' he said after a pause. The involuntary distaste in his face at mention of his wife turned to grimness. 'Dear Esmé.' He smiled, not pleasantly. 'A year ago, over a year ago, she got word of an affair I had and blew it up to an intended marriage. I've let her yap about it, she wasn't worth contradicting—then.' He shrugged. 'That whole affair, incidentally, was a mistake from beginning to end.'

His look was forbidding, his silence a chasm between them. Across it she offered a forlorn propitiation in a gesture long forgotten—of holding out her arms to a man. The clearing of his face was a rebirth. 'You fool,' he laughed, and hurt her with his embrace and ruthless kiss —an interval terminated by both of them with a curious simultaneousness of awakening, a caution ignoble yet obligatory.

'You're quite right,' he agreed, though she had said nothing. 'Not here.' He let her withdraw from his arms completely and watched her standing awkward and disoriented. His next words gave her a feeling of unrecognition; he had a cold and formidable power of detachment.

'You know my circumstances,' he said abruptly. 'My father—'

'Yes, yes.'

'And apart from my having to be with him we can't risk anything, not here.'

'Neither of us can,' she returned. 'I'd never let you take the chance, in any case.'

'If she smelled it out . . .' Thinking aloud, he seemed hardly to have heard her. 'We'll have to wait.'

'Yes.'

'Very good then, my love.' He returned and smiled at her. 'That's that.'

Her own faint smile dissimulated an unforeseen hunger in her, sharp as a knife. *When did you begin to like me?* she longed to ask, with sudden devouring need for flattery and reassurance, after the long famine. *When did you begin to love me? Tell me, please tell me.*

'I liked you at once, you know,' he said, as if she had spoken aloud. 'You were so tranquil, and I needed tranquillity. That look of yours, quiet, dependable, welldisciplined—I took you for one of those nice middleaged young women.' His voice changed. 'But that morning, the scare over Chris, and you came back to the office afterward—'

To his words and inflection she could put no name, except that they were life-giving; with starved intentness she listened to someone speaking about her—*her*—with love.

'—and you stood there in the doorway, so pale, and

your hair on end, and such big terrified eyes.' He smiled again. 'And I thought, *Poor young thing, poor frightened young thing.*'

It was then, her assuaged heart said greedily. *It was then, then.*

'So it was then,' he said. 'It began then, I expect.'

'I loved you at once.—No!' she gainsaid clumsily. 'I mean, I knew at once I could love you, if—if things were favourable.'

His look, amiable yet slighting, reminded her that men had not the same relish for these minute dissections as women. Instead—

'I'll have to be in London in five weeks,' he offered. 'Will you meet me there?'

'I'll meet you whenever or wherever you say,' she returned over a withering heart; five weeks! 'Anywhere.'

'I'm there for a few nights, perhaps four—we could be together—?'

'Oh yes.—But your father?' she remembered suddenly. 'Will you be able—'

'There's that,' he agreed bleakly. 'But there's no telling exactly when. He's a very strong man, unluckily for him, and it may go on and on. Of course I'd write off the conference if he died at just that time, otherwise I'd go.' He was silent a moment. '*If by reason of strength they be fourscore years and ten, yet is their strength labour and sorrow.* I never realized exactly what that meant till I saw what's been happening to him, this last year.'

Before the timeless misfortune, irremediable and too profound for consolation, she was silent.

'You know, when I refused your resignation—' he had returned from the estrangement of care '—it wasn't officialese, it was because I didn't want you to go.'

'Tom.' She was abrupt for fear of lamentable obviousness. 'I've a little flat in Earl's Court, but I—I'm afraid we couldn't stop there.'

'Lord no,' he returned decisively. 'I want us to be together and not have to jump at every alarm. There're plenty of nice hotels in Knightsbridge.'

'Just so long as you don't think I'm disgustingly cautious—' she petitioned.

'Don't be an ass. After the divorce everything'll be different, but just now I'm being fairly disgusting myself.'

She was silent, smiling under the mingled rebuff and caress.

'Well,' he said on an accent of finality and touched her cheek. 'Well.' He withdrew his hand.

For a timeless pause she stood motionless, looking at the door that had closed after him. The joy of their encounter overshadowed by anxiety, the passion tainted with prudence, combined to subdue and trammel her—till a tidal surge of delicious selfishness wiped it all away. With idiotic rapture she turned her head from side to side slowly, dazed with the unfamiliarity of this familiar room. The bleached sterile neon poured like sunlight, the metal shelves might sprout primrose and daffodils without surprising her unduly. Then her mind shaped a word that frightened her into darting out her hand and clutching the shabby deal table, the only wooden thing in this metallic room. She must be sly and careful, walk softly lest she draw the eye of the malign watcher that loves to spoil things for people; not dare even to think the word *happiness*, let alone speak it.

Five weeks, became her litany; its response, *the pleasure deferred that maketh the heart grow sick.*

Yet at first she had taken pleasure—the strange pleasure of the masker—in their breakfast-time disguise of civility and impersonal good-mornings. In minutes, only in minutes, there would be the wild contact of lips, the painful grip of his arms that she felt long after he had released her . . . the image shook her with a crazy silent hilarity and a mad desire to explode into laughter at the breakfast table. How the dumbfounded faces would turn toward her; how specially petrified the replacement for Marcus, a prim elderly accountant named Fellowes. . . . Yet the cruelest problem between them had settled itself in a matter of days. Knowing that abandonment was not yet for them, they avoided touching each other by unanimous yet wordless consent. They allowed themselves short commons, a morning kiss self-consciously gentle; no more of bodies flung together, of longings to take refuge in each other followed by miniature deaths of denial. Under this regimen she knew him no more content than herself, and she was fiercely discontented. Her body, that came clamouring to life after long drouth, racked her with a cruelty for which she was unprepared; beside the headaches and unease of this fever another uneasiness rode her, diffused but equally desolating. *Hurry, hurry,* she whimpered at crawling time, *Oh hurry, damn you, hurry.* Needing only patience and common sense, all the more fiercely she spurned them; she had been patient and sensible for long enough, too long. In this erosion she came at last to regard these days of postponement and severance with fear, superstitious fear; not only as loss and injury in themselves, but as indecipherable portents of danger.

'Your friend,' observed Mrs. Lees-Milburn, 'seems to have two strings to her bow.'

Alison roused from the narcotic preoccupation that
shut her from the outer world nowadays, and offered
a listless, 'Sorry—?'

'Your *friend*.' The old woman gave the noun its usual
poisonous inflection. 'Flourishing like the green bay tree.'

'Oh,' murmured the other, waking up. 'Well, more
power to her.' Ignoring Mrs. Lees-Milburn's offended
sniff, she bestowed a vague amused survey upon Myra's
present and sensational burgeoning. It had transpired
that the newcomer, Mr. Fellowes, was as ardent a bridge
player as the Major, as much dependent on it, and as
good a player; moreover he had engaged Myra for part-
nerships at his own club which met at a Folkestone hotel
instead of at W.I. rooms, and was consequently a rather
smarter club than the Major's. The Major in turn, roused
by this invasion of his once-exclusive territory, had been
driven to such desperate repelling tactics as inviting
Myra to the cinema, an event unprecedented in the
annals of Mowbray's.

'Dolling herself up as she does to go to these scruffy
little clubs,' said the old woman. 'Ridiculous.'

The virulent sneer switched her attention abruptly to
something other than the Major's defensive measures,
and much less amusing. This bitter and unrelenting
hostility between the two women; curious that it could
go on and on yet never once break surface, or not so far
as she knew; it might be less wearing to have it flare once
in a while, rather than this eternal smouldering. For her
own part, she had not a vestige of antagonism toward
Myra; in spite of past events she was pleased to see her
on top of her form and more in demand than ever. . . .

'She hasn't given up hope, that one,' Mrs. Lees-
Milburn declared. 'She'll nail one or other of those dry

old sticks before long, mark my words. And do you know, I can see either of 'em marrying her, just to make sure of a bridge partner.' She cackled malevolently. 'In exactly the way that infirm old men marry their nurses and housekeepers.'

Across the topic of Myra fell a new realization. Mrs. Lees-Milburn must be torn with anxiety against the day when Caroline, according to her warning, would be forced to raise her prices. The time was not yet apparently or else Caroline—superb symbol of the class extinguished by the MacDonalds and Bondfields of their day, and with such smug self-congratulation—was staving it off till the last possible moment. Yet, with this major worry gnawing at her, the old woman's hatred of Myra continued to flourish as rankly as if it were her sole preoccupation. People were strange, dauntingly, endlessly strange. . . . By the way, she had never again referred to having the hoard in her trunk examined. Either she had changed her mind or forgotten her fleeting idea, alcoholic. . . . . .

The letter that came in the morning post dealt her so heavy a blow that she saw how it attracted his attention across the breakfast table—his one quick glance at her stricken face, and his abstraction thereafter. When she marched into his office a little later she answered the question in his face before he had said a word.

'Our date,' she blurted. 'Our London thing.'

'What's wrong—?'

'Chris is coming,' she returned despairingly. 'For some project at the Science Museum, he's got special permission. Coming, and,' she added bitterly, 'bringing a friend with him.'

'Well,' he said after a moment; a light had gone out of him. 'Nothing to do about it. Another time then, that's all—we'll wait.'

'No, no, you don't understand, I—I've put him off, in a way.' She was shamefaced as if caught in something shameful. 'I mean, he knows I can arrange to come up, I've told him often enough—in my own stupid letters. And I haven't seen him since that—that accident horror, only rung him a couple of times. He wouldn't understand my not turning up at the flat, and—and I couldn't bear not to see him, I couldn't bear it.'

'Of course,' he concurred. 'Naturally—'

'No, but wait, wait,' she besought. 'I've sent him a note to say I couldn't possibly arrive when he did, but I'd come two days later. So instead of having four days together, we'll have two. If you—if you don't mind too much? It was the best I could do—?'

He rose unhurriedly from his desk, motioned, and followed her to the inner room.

'Don't be angry,' she said abjectly as soon as the door closed. 'Please don't be angry.'

For answer he put his arms around her and for a long moment held her, simply held her; in the enfolding gentleness and reassurance she felt her face going ugly with a sob.

'If anyone had told me,' she managed in a strangled voice, 'that I'd put off Chris for anyone on earth—!'

'Don't cry,' he said, releasing her. 'Anyway, you and Chris can have dinner with me, on the last two evenings?'

'Oh lovely.' He had transformed the severance into festivity. 'Lovely, lovely.'

'He might as well,' Durant added casually, 'meet his new father then as later.'

'Oh,' she returned after a moment, horridly demure.

The warmth he had rekindled in her surged to a dizzying, unbearable joy. 'You hadn't mentioned that.'

'I hear you when you don't speak aloud,' he reproved her amiably. 'You might return the compliment now and again.'

I love you, darling Tom, silently she tried the new word, staring at him. *I love you, I love you.*

'I too,' he murmured, and her enclosing joy was threaded with awe. This beautiful and distinguished man and this silent bond of communication between them; this spiritual fusion that was a feminine longing seldom realized. . . . 'You'll have Christmas dinner with us at the flat,' she said, all illumined with the idea, then remembered to add, 'If you can.'

He was turning toward the door when she said hastily, 'Don't go yet, I just wanted to ask you—'

'Yes?'

'I mean, I've been wondering. The library, and the tremendous budget you need for its upkeep—' odd moment for such an enquiry, yet with their new relationship she could ask; she had been curious for too long. 'I quite understand that your regulations wouldn't let you sell books, or manuscripts—'

'No, they wouldn't,' he said as she paused.

'No. But supposing, among the stuff you buy or inherit, there should be old letters with—with valuable stamps—'

His face had changed, a change invisible except to someone intimate with him; after a moment he asked, 'What put stamps into your head all at once?'

'Well, it's possible,' she countered speciously. 'In any library from an old house, I'd always expect to find letters stuck away and forgotten. Would they—the Governors —let you sell stamps, if you found any?'

'They'd be delighted to sell, it'd be found money—a windfall. Stamps are outside our province, we've never made collections and don't expect to do.' Still with that difference in his eyes and voice he repeated, 'What made you think of stamps?'

'Nothing,' she lied. 'It's just an idea.'

'Well, perhaps you'll find us a . . . what is it? the one-cent British Guiana, eighteen-fifty-something? and make our fortune.' His smile also had an indefinable quality, disconcerting. 'Keep an eye out for us.'

From a red-hot bath she returned to her room, red-hot from the gas-fire stoked with prodigal shillings, then took off her robe before the mirror and interrogated the luminous irradiation of her flesh. Yes, decidedly she could see the reward of her abstemiousness, with the inevitable result that she looked younger; her healthy solid body had become insupportable to her as an early aftermath of their first kiss. Her dormant vanity, after all these years, had come to life as ragingly as her senses; for him she wanted to be young and elegant, for him she aspired to a thousand things she had forgotten completely . . .

'Oh God, I'm happy,' she thought, then realized she had not thought it, she had said the dangerous word aloud. And said it, moreover, without fear, the fear that was cringing propitiation of Them, always waiting to destroy happiness. And this loss of fear was marvelous liberation, it was the falling of a weight off her neck; from being always afraid she breathed freely—for the first time—in the atmosphere of happiness, she confronted the prospect of happiness with serene assurance and expectation.

She put on her discreet black dinner dress, noting with pleasure that it caved in here and there where previously she had filled it out with no room to spare, and went down to dinner a trifle late; the others were already seated. As she took her place Mrs. Lees-Milburn, pleasurably big with event, trumpeted at her across the table, 'Well! we shan't be seeing much of Tom Durant from now on.'

The constriction of her heart had no time to shape an involuntary, *Oh God, what? some accident?*

'He's just rung Caroline,' the sybil was announcing, with funereal relish. 'Michael Durant died an hour ago.'

XIII

After dinner, depriving herself of coffee and Mrs. Lees-Milburn of a session for chewing over the mortuary tidbit, she fled to her room: she wanted to think. Undressing, taking off garment after garment slowly and automatically, she was thickly wrapped about with a calculation that excluded all else. The news had quickened her with plans, sent her thoughts racing in unforeseen channels. This death, expected a long time, meant release for Michael Durant; for his son grief undoubtedly, but release no less. And for herself—only she would not admit it in words—it meant the certainty that now they would meet in London; now there was no impediment any more, no obstacle to prevent . . .

Her look was still remote but her movements picked up the tempo of purpose. This was midweek; her time was reasonably at her disposal, and she had not lifted her nose from the grindstone since her arrival. The vacuum of Tom's absence she would use by going to London tomorrow, withdrawing some hoarded savings, and going shopping. This extravagance, and her first cold misgiving at the thought of it, was quickly followed by delicious reassurance. No longer had she so urgently to count every penny; she must get used to the idea.

Her face cleared with the clearing of conscience and the ordering of her agreeable plans. London tomorrow; this would give her two full days of shopping, counting

Saturday morning. Also the flat would take no harm from a little attention after two months of being shut up, her trip was necessary if only to prepare the flat for Chris and his friend. . . . A laugh escaped her at her own hypocrisy. She must learn not to dissimulate pleasure behind the mask of duty, her bright horizon made it no longer necessary; she must accustom herself to the idea of pleasure for pleasure's sake. . . .

Her gaze returned from indwelling to encounter—then focus upon—her pudding-basin hat. Picking up the blameless object that had done her long and faithful service, she eyes it with incredulous loathing. Was it possible that any woman in her senses should deform herself beneath such a horror, less caricature than insult? Throwing it on the floor she stepped deliberately upon it, then picked it up and scaled it like a schoolgirl to the top of the wardrobe. Then with her hoydenish gesture a shame fell upon her, a vestigial restraint. A man had just died a hard death after prolonged and terrible pain, and her response to this death was to caper like a released colt . . .

No, no, that was false, a die-hard convention of her false upbringing. She could have no feeling for old Mr. Durant, a man she had never seen. Her joy—her grateful joy—was not flaunted in the face of death, only offered in thanksgiving to her new life, to the power that had transformed her from a drudging machine to a woman giving herself for love. . . .

She tumbled into bed and into thrilling decision, simultaneously. Take the noon train tomorrow, take the latest train back on Sunday and be at Mowbray's just on midnight. Drifting into sleep she smiled with anticipation, with love and safety and lulling content.

The admirable service restored her to Folkestone according to calculation, triumphant with success and not

in the least tired. No porters at this hour, naturally, but
she was perfectly happy to manhandle a hatbox and her
biggest case, now considerably heavier than when she
had left. A taxi rattled her home through pitch-dark
countryside, houses all dark or with a single window
sleepily lit; she gave herself passively to the vibration
and to a momentary somnolence vacant with well-being.
The driver carried her case up the steps without being
asked; an elderly man with the old-fashioned politeness
and geniality, and tipping him lavishly was all part of the
joy. She let herself in softly, put out the light left on for
her benefit, and on tiptoe humped her burdens upstairs.
In this homecoming was a central hollowness, since the
house was empty of the one central being: he must still
be away, for days yet perhaps . . . . it only meant she had
his return to look forward to. The faint shadow passed;
she was happy again, excited and absurdly eager to get
her purchases out before they creased; review her booty
and the rightness of her choice . . .

Instantly on closing the door she flew at the case and
lifted out the first trophy, encapsuled as it had left the
shop; feverishly she acccleiated the rape of its pure fresh
tissue, then held it against herself and anxiously interrogated the mirror. A really good woollen dress, a beautiful shade of blue; of course by this light . . . yet even
while reserving judgment she had dug from the case a
suit, a coat, a satin blouse in brilliant purple, their wrappings whipping about like gigantic snowflakes. The hat
came out of the box for its moment of admiration and
trial; if it looked this good framing a face unmade-up
and a trifle weary. . . . Not that she was tired in the
least, on the contrary she was electrically wide-awake,
but it was latish and she had been cleaning the flat all
day Sunday to make up for her spree; even a hot bath

immediately after had not removed the spiritual grime of housework. . . . .

Then and later she could never decide if the talking in the hall had penetrated her envelope of obliviousness, or not. What with new finery and the festive rustling of tissue-paper, if she had heard it at all it was inattentively, without surprise. Others were up late, after all it was only a little past midnight. . . .

The first clutch of alarm came when the sound of voices, low and indistinct, was broken by a cry—brief and not loud, but enough to transfix her with sudden strained listening as she stood there, the new hat still in her hand. A cry of . . . fear? surprise? but no time to speculate, for the strange sound was succeeded by one even stranger, the thud of running feet, an irrhythmic padding soft yet violent. People running in bedroom slippers, more than one person . . . the confused trampling, brief as the cry that had preceded it, was cut short by a sound, horrible even through the closed door; a single impact brittle yet pulpy, and together with it an inhuman shriek, an outcry of raw terror, outrage, pain. . . . .

Witless and rooted, suddenly cold all over, she stood listening. Sounds arose outside, a babel of shock, query, consternation, louder and louder . . . . she put down the hat and nerved herself to open the door and peer out. Someone had turned on the big overhead chandelier, never used; by its harsh light the hall was confusingly full of figures in bathrobes, figures moving or standing or stooping. . . . After a moment she ventured just outside and gaped, idiotic, at the elements of the uproar: Mrs. Lees-Milburn lying across the threshold of her room with a dark outpouring from the side of her head that turned the shoulder of her bathrobe sodden black; Myra, standing like a statue, with something gripped in

her hand. Belatedly Alison recognized it as a fragment
of one of the blue vases on the hall table, a fragment still
clutched by its neck, but its lower end broken and
jagged. Remembering vividly the weight of it in her
hand, the solidity of the base, she was knifed by a cold
shiver while staring blankly at Myra—Myra now returning from her trance, with the movements of an autom-
aton. With no change whatever in her empty eyes and
empty face, with an air of absolute detachment, she let
the vase fall and turned her back unhurriedly on all of
them; walked unhurriedly into her room, and closed the
door. Nobody tried to prevent; all the flurry centered on
the blood-soaked figure within the door-frame and the
two men bending over her, trying to staunch the wound
with towels but patently not daring to move her. One of
the men straightened; even in this macabre moment, her
heart lurched. He was back, he had come back after
all . . .

As she stared at him he moved further into the hall,
and even this early an unease touched her, a full stop of
unrecognition. His colour was frightful, between yellow
and gray, and not from the pitiless lighting, she was somehow certain. And he must see her standing there, yet refused to glance her way even once . . . surely it was
overdoing discretion, that for one moment's comfort they
could not even look at each other . . . ?

'Miss Pendrell.'

She jumped at the brusque voice and turned her glance
upon the speaker; startled, yet relieved to free her eyes
from that avoidance, that stony unrecognition.

'Miss Pendrell,' Major Grant was repeating. 'You can't
do any good out here, perhaps you'd better just stop in
your room till the ambulance and police arrive. No help

to them to find too many people milling about, so just for the time being? if you don't mind—?'

Without even a gesture he had herded her backward into her room. Crisis had invested him with an old habit of military authority difficult to oppose; far from wishing to oppose it, she felt a cowardly gratitude at being screened from ugliness.

As he closed the door firmly upon her banishment, slowly she moved to a chair and slowly sat down; from her depth of profound shock and bewilderment canvassing her impressions. Tom's ghastly pallor, his lightless eyes refusing to meet hers, his bleak disowning face . . . and perforce she admitted his look for what it was, the look of calamity. Abysmally nonplussed, she set herself to conjecture its source. His wife, naturally; some new successful malignance of hers, and whatever it was, he was taking it hard. She would have to combat this despair and persuade him that marriage—for her—was a devalued coin; that so long as they were together all else was unimportant, immaterial. . . . .

Her eyes shot abruptly to the door. From beyond it came different sounds, of alien presences in the house— heavy footfalls on the stairs, a stranger's voice, brief and not loud; even at this remove its accent of authority taking over was unmistakable. Then came a long pause when she listened hard but to little effect; she could imagine what was going on but could hear nothing beyond vague continuous movement and talking. During this listening trance she had also been aware of a car or cars pulling up in front . . . . she hurried to a window and separated the curtains; although on the side of the house she should be able to see the ambulance lights flashing . . . not yet, apparently. With all her heart she

willed it to hurry, the poor old thing sprawled on the
floor could afford no margin of delay. . . .

She let the curtains fall and again confronted the blank
door and the ominous stir going on and on beyond it.
Her room was chaotic, drifts of tissue and gay new
clothes scattered about . . . to save her soul she could
not restore order, not just yet; the weakness of shock combined with her own bewilderments plucked at her nerves
and drove her into an aimless prowling, checked by the
faint sound of gravel crunching under a heavy vehicle.
She darted to the window again; this time a revolving
blue flash rhythmically broke and restored darkness. The
opening of the hall door was sensed rather than heard,
but the muffled tramplings of people coming upstairs was
plain enough. . . .

At this instant another sound transfixed her; a whoop-
ing or retching terrible in its violence, along with a new
clamour of voices mounting in new emergency. The
retching went on and on, unbearable in its extremity of
distress, leaving her shrivelled to nothing before authen-
tic disaster. Cruel that Mrs. Lees-Milburn had had to come
to before they took her away, cruel and horrible that the
proud masterful old woman could not have remained unconscious for another while at least. . . .

She might open the door, for only one quick glance?
At once she decided otherwise—not from Major Grant's
prohibition, but the mean peering curiosity of it. Meanwhile, from the hall, came indications that the situation
was being mastered, as with most situations however
dire; the spasmic gagging faded away and was followed
by heavy laden sounds going downstairs, irregular shuf-
flings, then silence. No, not silence, not real silence. A
residue of disturbance was left, the sense rather than
sound of something still imminent . . .

It came, and made her jump; the knocking had been soft and discreet, yet unmistakably official. She went to open, finding what she expected, but not in uniform; an affable man, rather young.

'May I have your name, madam?' he asked politely. 'And you spell that . . . Thank you. Now the Detective-Inspector will wish to see you presently?' he appended, 'so if you'd mind not going to bed till he does do?'

'All right,' she agreed. 'I shan't.'

'Sorry for the inconvenience,' he went on as if she had protested. 'But easier for you to stop up, h'm, then being knocked up out of your sleep?'

'When do you expect he'll want me?' she asked.

'When he gets around to you,' he answered her as she deserved. 'It's not very comfortable for anyone, but you know how it is.'

He won't get much out of me, your Detective-Inspector, she informed him with grim triumph as the door closed. *I've been away. I'm out of all this, thank God, well and truly out of it.*

After a moment she set about tidying the room; soberly hanging away the new clothes she had been gloating over with such joyful vanity, and folding the scattered paper with absurd precautions against its rustling. Then for a moment she stood thinking of the next thing, the prospect of the official summons; she had better remain fully dressed. Stopping only to change her shoes to bed-room slippers she lay down with the bedspread for cover and at once was shaking with mortal chill. That man in the hall whom she knew—whom she thought she knew— as Thomas Durant; his stricken pallor, his sightless eyes averted from her . . . and she, bewildered and desolate for comfort, unable to go now and knock at his door for one solacing word or glance. Impossible even under best conditions in Caroline's house—let alone now, when every separate floor must be under surveillance and every separate dweller penned separately in his cubicle, till authority should require him . . . she shivered again, this time with devastation of the unfamiliar, the destroyingly alien. Daily appearance, daily custom, solid as rock: how fragile actually, how easily shifted and tilted by one finger-tap of catastrophe. She and everyone in this house jerked from their peaceful orderly grooves of existence, lined up to await, in a dire equality, the first inquisitions of the law. . . .

The knocking, soft and considerate as before, again had the underlying accent that brought her galvanically from her doze. She started up, got her feet on the floor, and stood.

'Yes,' she called in an unwoken voice, 'Yes,' then saw across the room a pale face with eldritch hair. Snatching an instant to take up a comb, *They won't care how you look*, she thought, and opened the door upon the same officer and his same courteous manner, deprecating. Stepping into the hall, she had a half-glimpse of a faded old bathrobe disappearing unsteadily up the stairs to the second floor; only one person lived up there. Poor Caroline, what had she done to deserve this profanation of her shrine still inhabited by her husband and son. . . . As she followed the man down she had another vision; this houseful of ghosts in bathrobes, walking at unearthly hours to face the utmost rigours of questioning; elderly ghosts needing their night's sleep, and their sleep hopelessly broken. And the silence as profound as if it had never been ruptured; the emptiness unpeopled, except for that glimpse of Caroline's unsteady back. . . .

'What time is it?' she asked huskily by a sort of reflex, and he answered, 'Quarter to three.'

He had already opened the door for her, politely, and she passed into the lounge.

Contact with any degree of the higher police lay beyond her experience and imagination both; such relationships were limited, on her part, to affable 'good-days' exchanged with the neighborhood constable whom she knew by sight. Of the man who half-rose at her entrance and sat down again without wasting time, she could get no impression but the obvious unimportant kind. He was almost middle-aged, square-set but not fat, with unmemorable features in a squarish face. Normally he would be fresh-complexioned, she guessed, but a sort of grayness underlay his healthy colour at the moment. Fatigue, of course, and the rasp in his voice as he spoke was probably not bad temper nor impatience, but also fatigue. His suit—not good and not bad, she noted vaguely—contributed to his faceless respectability; he merely looked like a reliable type with a job to do and every intention of doing it.

She sat down at his invitation; he looked at some notes and rehearsed her name, address, marital status, how long she had been at Mowbray's—

'About two months,' she heard herself saying, and was surprised. That long a time? so long, so short . . . ?

'Please—' she blurted involuntarily as he put down his notes and readied himself for the work in hand. '—I only wanted to ask,' she continued as he paused '—how is Mrs. Lees-Milburn?'

'They don't know yet,' he returned grudgingly.

'I mean, will she recover—?'

'A woman that old?' He shrugged. 'Taking a knock on
the head like that, then the shock with it—?'

'She's strong.' Was she opposing his pessimism out of
concern for Mrs. Lees-Milburn, or to delay the questioning? 'She's got a wonderful constitution.'

'She must have, or she wouldn't be alive now.' He was
expressionless. 'But as I've told you, they aren't committing themselves yet.—Now, Miss Pendrell.' He transfixed her with a different look and tone. 'This business
upstairs—what do you know about it?'

'Nothing,' she returned crisply. His question reinforced,
with granite, all her resolution of detachment. 'I've been
in London since Thursday afternoon, I took the 10.10
from Charing Cross this evening, and taxied here from
Folkestone just on midnight. I hadn't been in my room
ten minutes, actually I'd started to unpack, when the—
the commotion broke out.'

'You saw something directly,' he countered. 'You came
into the hall after it happened.'

'I opened my door,' she contradicted as positively.
'And hardly moved beyond it. I saw Mrs. Lees-Milburn
on the floor and a lot of confusion. I'd no time to sort it
out—Major Grant made me go back. So I did,' she confronted him with the boldness of candour. 'I went back.'

'And that's all you know of it—?'

'Absolutely all.' *For anything you get out of me*, she
told him silently, *I'll give you full marks*. 'By the way,'
she said as if on sudden recollection, and with spurious
helpfulness offered him something of no value. 'I did
hear a very slight sound of voices just before the incident,
but whose I couldn't tell you—I was unpacking and took
no notice.'

'I see.' His accent was of tired acceptance; she congratulated herself on her tactics.

'How well,' he essayed, 'did you know Mrs. Lees-Milburn?'

'As well as one does after a few weeks, in a place like this,' she returned. 'Old-fashioned gentry of her type don't pick up close friends in boarding-houses.'

'Oh,' he grunted, again on the tone of checkmate; elevated by success, she ventured a suggestion.

'Mrs. Mowbray has known Mrs. Lees-Milburn all her life,' she offered. 'She's the one that can tell you all about her.'

His expression changed, and not for the better; seeing her mistake too late, she quailed in advance. *I didn't ask you what Mrs. Mowbray knows, I asked you what you knew*, was as plain in his face as if spoken. Yet his obvious intention of snubbing her was—for some reason—withheld or postponed; suddenly, his face changing again, he made a curious digression. 'In your opinion, Miss Pendrell: would Mrs. Mowbray take exception to . . . ah . . . irregularities among her guests, even discreet irregularities? or not?'

'Good heavens.' She regarded him open-mouthed, shaken by mere surprise into truthfulness. 'If I understand what you mean by irregularities, I shouldn't expect her to put up with anything like that, not for a single moment.' Myra, she thought, some pitiful little affair of Myra's upheaved to the surface in the course of the greater upheaval? Some clandestine relationship with . . . the correct and wooden Major? the prim and proper Mr. Fellowes . . . ? 'She'd never stand for it,' she added. 'Discretion or no discretion.' *Poor Myra*, lamented unceasingly through her mind, *poor, poor Myra. . . .*

'Have you just remembered something?' he asked mildly.

'No.' She came to with a start. 'Why?'

'You look as if you'd just thought of something.'

'Yes,' she lied. 'I was thinking what a pity that that poor old woman had to recover consciousness, before they took her away. Such pain she must have been in by the—the sounds she was making. Horrible,' she murmured faintly. 'Horrible.'

'She didn't recover consciousness.' He was too explicit somehow. 'Mrs. Lees-Milburn wasn't making those sounds.'

'But who . . . . ?'

'Miss MacKinnon,' he informed her. 'She went back to her room after the assault—and you saw her,' he accused vindictively. 'You were standing there, you saw her, and you just let her walk away.'

'But I saw her just for a moment,' she protested in bewilderment. 'The Major made me go back—I told you.'

'Well, at any rate she went straight into her room—' he ignored her excuse '—and swallowed something.'

'Oh no,' she moaned after a moment. 'Oh no, no.'

'The stuff'd just begun to take hold when the ambulance and doctor came for the old lady. Otherwise,' he stated grimly, 'she'd be dead now.'

She sat quiet, completely crushed.

'How well—' he had no mercy on her '—did you know Miss MacKinnon?'

'Quite well.' Even through her horror, the query stiffened all her determination to keep out of it. 'We were at Somerville together.'

'So you're old friends.'

'In a way.' She rallied enough to digress. 'How is—how is Miss MacKinnon?'

'They don't know that either, not as yet.—Now I understand from others here—' he was watching her with unpleasant fixity, or did she imagine it? '—that she and the old lady weren't on good terms.'

'Perhaps not,' she conceded indifferently. 'I suppose they weren't.'

'And your *friend* Miss MacKinnon never discussed this situation with you—?'

'Oh, she . . . tried more than once. Or rather she felt her way toward trying. Guest-house backbiting.' She grimaced dismissively. 'I wasn't being drawn into that. Anyway,' she summed up, 'apart from Mrs. Mowbray, I should say that Mrs. Lees-Milburn despised pretty much everyone here.'

She had defeated him; he had to surmount the full stop of frustration before asking, 'So you can't give any reason for this attack on Mrs. Lees-Milburn by Miss Mac-Kinnon?'

She shook her head.

'Did it surprise you?' he queried oddly.

'Completely.' Here again she could afford to be honest. 'I mean, between two women like that I can imagine angry words, that sort of unpleasantness. But any-thing . . . murderous . . . like this—no, I can't make it out at all.'

'Well.' He looked so discouraged, and so tired, she could almost be sorry for him. 'I'd better let you go, h'm? We'd all be better for some sleep, I expect.'

She smiled, gently and submissively feminine.

'But first—' he was making a final effort, unmistakably, against his depletion '—on just one or two points, I'd be grateful for your opinion—just your opinion.'

'Of course,' she murmured cordially; out of her victory, she could spare him that much small change.

'We don't know why it actually happened, this business tonight.' He made the surprising statement in a voice

half-extinguished by fatigue and with eyes kept open by
main force. 'No one seems to know.' He paused again.
'Before Miss MacKinnon collapsed, she'd time to give us
two versions of the affair. But these two stories of hers—
they don't match.'

He was silent a moment, as if floored for once and all.

'Actually,' he plodded on, 'they contradict each other
at every point—every single detail. So where's that leave
us? We've got to establish motive, haven't we, before we
can move an inch? So—' undisguisedly he threw himself
on her mercy '—if I repeat these two stories to you, and
see which one strikes you as likeliest—?'

'Well,' she began dubiously.

'I know, I know,' he forestalled her. 'It's not what you
know for sure, it would just be your opinion. But even
that could throw some light somehow, somewhere—one
never knows. If you'd just listen,' he appealed, 'I'd take
it as a favour.'

'All right.' Her unpromising response concealed a sudden avid curiosity, mixed with a condescending compassion for this poor hack at the end of his resources.
'For what it's worth, I'll listen.'

'Thank you. Well, Miss MacKinnon's first account of
the matter—' he stifled an engulfing yawn '—her first story
was, that she'd got in the old lady's room. Not for the
purpose of taking anything, she says, just to try and have
a look at some stuff, documents or something, that were
stored in a trunk in there. She took this chance, she
claims, because the old lady'd got very deaf of late, and
this deafness made it a little less risky—'

Before the growing disbelief in her face he broke off
and queried, 'So far, you don't like it—?'

'The deafness part of it is all right.' She began to succumb, as once before, to the fascinating game of re-

construction and conjecture. 'Only I'd expect Mrs. Lees-Milburn to lock her door.'

'Miss MacKinnon claims she found it unlocked. A woman that old—she might forget to lock it, it's possible.'

'Yes, it's possible.' She thought a moment. 'How could Miss MacKinnon expect to find her way—see what she was doing?'

'There was a night light.'

'Oh.' Just in time she caught back the remembering betrayal of *Oh yes*. 'I see.'

'Well, there's not much more to it. The old lady woke up unexpectedly and challenged her—got out of bed and came toward her—and from sheer panic Miss MacKinnon grabbed the nearest object, unfortunately something pretty heavy, and hit her.'

'No,' she said instantly, before she could think.

The silence that stretched out, endless, was different from the silences preceding it. This silence was like a still, sinister beam of light, casting into relief the trip-wire she had approached with such unseeing confidence, and the headlong force with which it had thrown her.

XIV

'Continue, Miss Pendrell,' he invited softly. Without moving so much as an eyelid he was transformed—from a commonplace man sodden with tiredness to a hunter terrifyingly wide-awake and in sight of his quarry. If earlier she had had any doubts about his quality, now she had none at all; he was, quite simply, formidable.

'Just what did you mean,' he continued his gentle drilling at her live nerve of disaster, 'by no?'

'I mean—' she began, and swallowed. The damage was done, she had no choice but to go on. '—it didn't happen like that, in Mrs. Lees-Milburn's room. It couldn't have happened in there.'

'And why not?' he persisted, always with that frightening softness.

'Because that—that vase she was hit with—'

'How,' he interrupted, 'did you know it was a vase?'

'I saw it in Miss MacKinnon's hand,' she returned, 'when I looked out of my room.'

'You saw it in Miss MacKinnon's hand,' he echoed. 'Odd you didn't mention that before.'

'I've only now realized it,' she fended lamely. 'It's only just now come back to me.'

'I see.' His smile was anything but reassuring. 'Please go on.'

'Well, that vase—it was one of a matching group on the side-table in the hall—a vase on either side of the lamp. They've stood there always,' she laboured on. 'So one of them couldn't have been in Mrs. Lees-Milburn's room. So it follows—' she took a shaky breath '—that Miss MacKinnon couldn't have picked it up where she said.'

'The old lady,' he observed, 'might have borrowed the vase.'

She hardly paused before gainsaying, 'No.' Her accent of decision surprised her. 'What would she borrow it for, flowers? You'd have found them on the floor, wouldn't you? spilled water—?'

'There was nothing like that,' he admitted, 'in the room.'

'Anyway, both vases were standing there as usual when I came home.' The belated image was distinct in her mind, the hall softly illumined and orderly. 'They're very good Victorian glass, I'm rather conscious of them. If one had been missing I'm sure I'd have noticed the lopsided effect. No, the . . . the trouble—it happened in the hall. And Mrs. Lees-Milburn ran, and Miss MacKinnon went after her and caught her at the door of her room.' The pressure of certitude and its induced fluency ran her full tilt into another deadfall. 'Because I heard that much. I heard them running.'

'You heard them running,' he observed with deadly pleasantness. 'That's something else you didn't mention before.'

I forgot, she started to say, *it's only just come back to me.* The feeble excuses dwindled and died before the look he turned upon her—a look that might daunt a nature far more thick-skinned than her own.

'Miss Pendrell,' he began, after a weighted silence. 'From the moment you walked in here, you've been lying to me. Not directly, no, only by suppression and evasion, by withholding the truth. Now before we go on, in case you don't understand your position in the matter, I'll make it clear to you. If that old woman dies, and for my money there's little doubt she will die, what we're dealing with here is either murder or manslaughter. Murder,' he repeated, 'or manslaughter.'

The words dropped like lead; he let fall an equally leaden silence. Newspaper words, unreal, yet by mere sound infused with reality, even through a closed door. . . .

'You don't trifle with either of those,' he was saying. 'Unless you like the idea of being accessory to the fact. To mention just one item—' he fixed her with an unsparing eye '—every single person I've spoken to agrees that you were rather a favourite with Mrs. Lees-Milburn, certainly on good enough terms to take her out to dinner and so forth. Yet you've consistently represented yourself as not knowing her better than anyone here, which was grossly misleading. And not—' he regarded her inimically '—not your only attempt to suppress evidence, as it's turned out.' Again he punctuated his indictment with a lethal silence. 'In other words, what you've been impeding is either a murder or a manslaughter enquiry, as well as wasting my time. Now before we proceed, do you understand your obligations in this matter?'

'Yes,' she said humbly.

'Glad to hear it.' He was grim. 'Let's begin again, from the beginning.' He was grimmer. 'And this time, don't leave anything out.'

Fool, fool, what a fool she had been; she had had to be devious, she had had to be clever, and now found herself the object not only of a dangerous hostility, but probably of distrust as to every word she might say hereafter. Thanks entirely to herself, to her own efforts, *fool*. . . .

She roused from her self-excoriation to find him waiting; not impatiently, only implacably. Frightened by that massive attendance on her pleasure, nevertheless she took a flustered moment wondering where to start. How far back it had all begun, she realized with surprise; all the ant-hill heapings of dull days and trivial happenings, yet all of it mounting, looming, gathering toward the climax . . .

'In September I was offered a job in the library here, in connection with a bequest,' she began. 'It was coincidence that Miss MacKinnon worked in the same library. We'd always kept in touch more or less, and she was glad I was coming and so was I. And she was very kind, got me booked into Mowbray's by good luck—otherwise I might have had to stop in Folkestone.'

She drew a breath, unsteady.

'She remained perfectly cordial till it dawned on her that I was handling a job she'd always done till then— cataloguing newly-acquired material. Then she changed, straightaway,' she attempted inadequately. 'She resented it, very much. She made her resentment so plain that I— I went to Mr. Durant and offered him my resignation.' His mere name strengthened her; tomorrow she would see him, speak to him. . . .

'You offered your resignation to Mr. Durant,' her audience prompted.

'Yes,' she returned. 'He refused to accept it, so I stopped here.'

'He's your employer, Mr. Durant?' he pursued. 'Also Miss MacKinnon's?'

'Well, technically the library is our employer. Mr. Durant—' she repeated the name for comfort '—is head of Champernowne, and our superior officer.'

'And what—' he bypassed her exactitudes '—was Miss MacKinnon's attitude after that?'

'Progressively unfriendly,' she continued as bidden. 'Well, by then I'd picked up some odd rumours at the library—'

'Yes,' he whipped her faltering heels. 'Go on.'

'There was some gossip—only among junior staff, just the very junior,' she qualified hastily, 'a sort of impression that Miss MacKinnon, when classifying a previous bequest of books—had found an old letter with a valuable stamp, maybe more than one, and had taken them to London and sold them privately. At any rate, she came back with some clothes so obviously expensive they'd be bound to attract notice. This was before I came here, but,' she amplified, 'I do remember her as always dressing rather . . . well, between poorly and carelessly . . . and I expect she'd always dressed the same way here.'

'Private money?' he suggested. 'Inherited?'

'I shouldn't expect so, she's from very poor people in Glasgow. She'd never talk about her family at college, I remember. But if she'd come into money now, she'd be almost sure to brag—exaggerate the amount.' Meticulously she added, 'She'd exaggerate everything, always.'

'All right.' He had listened to her carefully. 'Now this library rumour—do you believe it?'

She hesitated.

'Or—' he helped her '—did you put some part of it down to loose talk?'

'I did, yes, perhaps most of it. Until—'

'Until?' he prodded.

'Oh dear,' she murmured in despair. 'I'll have to go back rather far.'

'Do that,' he agreed. 'Back to Adam if you like.'

'There was a man stopping in this house, whom Miss MacKinnon never spoke to,' she began. 'Not even good-morning. She kept telling me how awful he was, and she didn't understand Mrs. Mowbray's letting in such a type, and so on. But by chance I saw her with this man in a bar, talking very confidentially, and she knew I'd seen them.' She paused, feeling her way. 'So she admitted to me, I mean she had to admit, that there was some arrangement between them, he was paying her—or was going to pay her—for getting any sort of information, or finding any approach—to Mrs. Lees-Milburn.' She paused for breath. 'There're a lot of old papers she keeps in a trunk—'

He made a movement so sharp and sudden that involuntarily she stopped, looking at him with doglike uncertainty—a look he failed to return; his forehead was knotted, his eyes remote. 'Yes,' he said finally, not to her. 'Yes.'

He returned from far away, and at once—by some clairvoyance—it was plain to her that they were striking out a different line of country.

'Now,' he said, his look fixed on her even more implacably. 'Now, this trunk.'

He had taken the reins from her hands; docile, she waited.

'This trunk the old lady's got in her room,' he said. 'What do you know about it?'

'Only what I've heard her say,' she returned. 'It's her mother's correspondence with various literary figures of her day.'

'Would stuff like that have any value?'

'Oh yes.' Now on professional ground, unconsciously

she resumed the lead. 'Of course it would depend, but
unknown letters of that period, the Brownings, Tennyson,
Dickens—' she gestured '—American universities pay the
earth for things like that. Or there might be something
in there absolutely unique, that would make a very high
price if offered for sale. Impossible to tell,' she deprecated. 'Since no one's ever examined them.'

'Examined,' he grunted. 'From what I understand,
hardly anyone's seen the trunk, even.'

'I've seen it.'

'*You've* seen it—?'

'Mrs. Lees-Milburn showed it to me.' Suppose she tried
to hold back, again, something that would come out
later; for all her resentment of duress she dared not, she
had had her lesson.

'She thought someone had been in her room,' she continued. 'And asked me would I come in and see.'

'And had anyone been in there?' His voice had leaped,
his glance re-impaled her with sharper attention. 'In your
opinion—?'

'I'd never been in her room before,' she fended, 'so
I'd no way of comparing. But so far as I could see, there
was no . . . special disorder.'

'Go on,' he commanded.

'There's a cover on the trunk, and she thought someone had knocked it awry. I'm practically sure she'd done
it herself,' she explained, 'brushing past. So then she
opened the trunk—'

'*Opened* it?' he barked.

'Just for a moment,' she disclaimed anxiously. 'Just to
make sure nothing'd been disturbed, and obviously it
hadn't been. So she closed it again, and that was all.'

'But didn't you manage to see what she had in there?
not anything?'

'In a split second, and by poor light?' she rebutted. 'I saw bundles of old envelopes and some faded writing, and that was all.'

'And you still think she imagined it—that someone'd been in her room?'

'I did then,' she answered blankly. 'And yes, I think I still do.'

'Do you?' in his look of grim humour—if it were humour—was no cordiality whatever. 'In this whole house no one's ever seen this legendary trunk but Mrs. Mowbray and her cleaner, and it's nothing to them but a piece of furniture. So I've actually met someone who's seen it, and seen it open at that.'

His accusation was so implicit that her brief composure vanished. Shaken again, seeking some means of propitiation, she remembered a stray item.

'I forgot to tell you,' she offered. 'That man that Miss MacKinnon said was after documents—well, I rang the V and A about him, and it turns out that he's actually a dealer in stamps.'

'Stamps—?' He had come to life with a sort of incandescent fury; if documents meant little to him, valuable stamps he could understand.

'And when he was here he called himself Marcus,' she added, out of sheer fright. 'But it seems his name's Braun.'

From the quality of the silence that followed, it was plain she could expect little good.

'All right, Miss Pendrell,' he spoke at last, on a slow grinding note. 'Here's this trunk. Maybe worth thousands. But no *maybe*,' he shot at her, 'about its being the centre of this whole business. Around this trunk there's been a constant stew and sweat of mystery, bribery, conspiracy, efforts to examine, a possible attempt at burglary. All this you've known all the time, and all this I've had to drag out of you bit by bit. You're the only person in this house who's not only seen the trunk open, but who has the best idea of its possible value. You're the one with the best knowledge of the two women involved, and with the best idea of the antagonism between them. The key to this affair—whatever key there is—at present you hold it. And you sit there telling me,' he exploded, 'you were in London, and knew nothing about it—!'

He broke off, trying to control himself; she had time for an even ampler view of her ruinous stupidity. This man, like most other people, lived by his record of performance. By trying to impede him, she had jeopardized his livelihood. She was his enemy, and was close to making him her enemy . . .

'Sorry, I'm very sorry,' she said humbly. 'I apologize.'

'Now.' He had not deigned to acknowledge her submission; he was too busy trying to surmount his rage. 'So far we have this old lady's trunk, of unknown value. We also have evidence of persistent attempts to get at it. We know likewise that Miss MacKinnon seems to be at the heart of these attempts, acting for this Braun, but also acting maybe—for a principal who hasn't yet appeared. Does that suggest anyone to you?' He was watching her closely. 'Someone nearer to home than Braun?'

Across her horizon the Major flitted intangibly, but remained intangible.

'No,' she answered.

'You're sure—?'

She shook her head with bewilderment so patent it seemed to satisfy him.

'All right,' he continued. His voice, worn and ragged, was also a voice with no intention of giving up. 'Now Miss MacKinnon's first account of this shindy—that it took place in the old lady's room—you've put it out of court with your story about the vase. It couldn't have happened in the room. It did take place in the hall.'

He fixed her with an enigmatic look; she returned it blankly.

'Which brings us,' he appended, 'to Miss MacKinnon's second account of what happened.'

During an interval, rumination closed him in again; he sat for moments before repeating, in a voice of soliloquy, 'Motive.'

For no reason, she hardly dared breathe.

'Find motive,' he pursued, 'and you clear up the whole picture, usually. But now you're going to see, Miss Pendrell—' he had returned to awareness of her '—how completely these two yarns of Miss MacKinnon's contradict each other. On everything, but especially on motive.'

She said nothing; her look of attention, painfully riveted, said all.

'This second version of hers is,' he bore on, 'that she was leaving a certain gentleman's room just after midnight, and Mrs. Lees-Milburn saw her. She says she'd looked first, made certain the coast was clear, and the hall did appear to be empty. But the old lady was there all the time, standing back in her own doorway and keeping quiet. Whether deliberately, or because she just happened to be going to the lavatory, we'll probably never know. Miss MacKinnon seemed to imply it was deliberate.'

He paused; no sound nor motion of hers broke the pause.

'Well, you can imagine how it was with the poor young woman—appalled, just standing there paralyzed and no way out of it. And the old lady came up to her—smiling,

Miss MacKinnon described it—and said, "By eight tomorrow morning, everyone in this house will know."'

During another silence, the picture of gloating cruelty —unbearably vivid in her mind—was also true to persons and circumstances. It sounded like Mrs. Lees-Milburn; it was in character.

'And then . . . ?' she barely achieved a whisper.

'Well then, she says she implored the old woman not to give her away—begged, pleaded, all but went on her knees—and the other just started laughing. And then, Miss MacKinnon says, something snapped—just gave way inside her head, and that's the last she knew. Doesn't remember picking up the vase or going after the old woman—doesn't remember anything.'

He let pass another moment, brief yet heavy—heavy as the vase on the old head—before asking, 'How does it sound to you? how plausible?'

'It . . . ties in with what I heard from my room.' Her hesitation was no longer of reluctance or evasion, only of carefullest consideration. 'Voices, then running, then the—the sound of the blow.'

'But apart from all that' He was impatient. 'Would that particular situation be enough to drive Miss MacKinnon into doing what she did? D'you find it enough motive to account for violence like that? A murderous attack?'

While she weighed this, he attended with respect; obviously he was expert in assessing the use made of silences.

'I don't know,' she groped finally. 'When I first knew her—of course it was years ago—'

'It may be relevant,' he urged as she came to a stop. 'Go on.'

'I . . . I wish . . .'

'You wish? What?'

'I wish I could make Myra plain to you, as she was then.' She was remote, almost wistful. 'A brilliant girl from a working-class family in actual poverty, I should think, and *poisoned*—literally—by the thought of her origins. Some people will always laugh at these distinctions, I expect, but others will always mind. She was one that minded, frightfully. For instance, we'd girls at Somerville with handles to their names, and she'd go out of her way to be offensive to them, really offensive. But apart from that one thing, she was such fun to know. So . . . so alive. So unusually pretty too, and amusing—and so full of hope, absolutely on fire with hope. And daring at games, she'd take risks and incur reproofs—but not too many, she was at college on a scholarship, she couldn't risk losing that for mere stunts—'

'Go on.'

'—and she was generous too. Not with money of course, she was poor, but any other way she could help you, she'd turn herself inside out to do it. So a person like Myra—'

Her voice, from its store of conclusion, gained new force.

'—a person who'd pulled herself by her bootstraps out of a world she hated, into a world much higher, socially and professionally—yes, I can see her fighting for it tooth and nail. Because if she lost that, she'd lose everything. She'd worked hard for it, it was literally all she had. Just to show you the extent of her attitude—'

'Yes?' he encouraged.

'Well of course she's a desperate snob, one knows that from college days. An inverted one—?' She smiled painfully. 'Every group on earth has its snobs, I expect, and Myra is a library snob. For example, she'd never put in

for a public library job if she could help it. She'd want
to be with some distinguished private foundation like
the Champernowne, or with a library attached to a
museum, something like that. It all goes to show how
hard, how very very hard, she takes these distinctions.
So—' she drew breath, the deepest yet '—so if all that were
threatened, I expect it's quite possible she might go ber-
serk like that, just . . . *break*. Because Mrs. Mowbray'd
ask her to leave, that's one sure thing. The old lady would
have spread the story far and wide, that's another. And
it's quite possible she'd lose her job and—' her voice
wavered up the graph-line of trouble '—and be followed
by this thing wherever she applied for work. The librarians' world is a small one, it still has old-fashioned stand-
ards, requirements . . .'

He attended on this recital with a look increasingly
. . . sardonic, was it? A strange look at any rate, unless
it were a trick of her eyes, tired and blinking from the
harsh overhead light.

'I've thought of something else,' she blurted, surprising herself.

'Yes?'

'Myra . . . was seen coming out of a man's room? at
midnight, you said? Only, if it was midnight—' arithmetic
had dispelled her weariness '—she'd have gone in there
perhaps at ten. But how insanely risky,' she argued. 'To
try anything of that sort, surely you'd wait till *after* midnight, then slip back at three or four? The timing, something about the . . .' she probed incoherently ' . . . the
timing's wrong.'

'I don't say it mightn't be, in the case of a younger
man.' His amusement gleamed dark and baleful. 'But
once you get past all that sizzling youth, you're not up
to all-night sports and grabbing a couple of hours' sleep

between dawn and seven. You settle for something less ambitious—have your bit of fun, but have your night's sleep too.'

He was only just not smiling; she would have disliked him if not for the pathetic image he had created. Poor, poor Myra, snatching at romance and involving in her act one or other of those respectable elderly men in a shaming ridiculous situation . . . the wooden Major? the prim and proper Mr. Fellowes? She recoiled even from conjecture; with all her heart she wanted not to know, seeing Myra clamped in monotony, the promise of her college days stopping dead in the tomblike library, the threepenny bridge and eventless days, months, years; Myra aware of looks slowly vanishing and mad for any change, anything different. . . .

And again, Myra's prospects from now on: Myra trapped by malice in a bad corner, Myra half-killing an old woman in consequence, then attempting suicide. . . . Deeply and unconsciously Alison sighed. Mrs. Lees-Milburn would die, being ninety, and Myra would recover, being thirty. Recover—for what? a public trial, a sentence? the horrors of imprisonment, for a violent nature like hers? And then? and after that . . . ?

'Well.' His intruding voice had made her start slightly. 'Well, you make it sound reasonable.'

For an instant, still immersed, she honestly made no sense of his slow considering words.

'Maybe you're right,' he went on ruminating. 'Maybe this threat to her standing, social, professional, would drive her up the wall so she'd smash in an old woman's head. But for myself—'

He dropped into discontented mutterings, no longer addressed to her.

'—no, that's not all of it. For me it doesn't explain . . .

doesn't begin to explain all of it. . . . No, there's something else. Something happened in that hall we don't know about . . . to make MacKinnon go crazy like that. . . .'

He abandoned soliloquy and looked at her. 'Anything else occur to you, above and beyond what you've told me? Anything at all—?'

Her blank head-shake seemed to convince him.

'Now why,' he demanded, 'didn't you come out with all this in the first place?'

'Because I didn't want to be involved,' she returned flatly.

'Was that the only reason?' he shot at her all at once. 'There wouldn't be some other reason?'

'What other . . .' she began, gaping at him; this veering about on a new tack, when she thought release was in sight, had shaken her witless. 'What other reason?'

'That you're protecting someone, eh? someone who hasn't yet appeared in all this? You wouldn't be protecting some such person—?'

'What person?'

Again her stare of bewilderment, approaching imbecility, seemed to convince him.

'Well.' The monosyllable seemed always to precede his trances of soliloquy, half-audible. 'MacKinnon . . . . now wait, wait. Maybe, just maybe—' his low voice quickened a little, spurred by some new idea. 'Those two stories of hers—could be that one doesn't exclude the other, necessarily. Could be that she gets around fast. She might've been in Durant's room first, then tried the old lady's room second. The trunk, it all comes back to the—'

'But—'

Completely absorbed, he did not so much ignore as fail to hear her.

'—the trunk, and someone knows what's in it. Or knows more than we've any idea of, as yet—'

'But—but—' The same astonishment that had ejected her first gasp forced out the second; only under such pressure would she have dared interrupt. '—that can't be —that's impossible.'

'What can't be?' He had made one of his lightning transfers of attention. 'What's impossible?'

'That she—that Myra—was in Mr. Durant's room. It's impossible.'

'Oh, she was in his room all right,' he said absently. 'He doesn't deny it.' Strangling a yawn, he got to his feet. 'Lord, quarter past four. And we needn't have been so late,' he rebuked her again, 'if only you'd cooperated—been frank from the begi-i-i—' He killed a second yawn. 'Sorry. By the way, I'm leaving a man on guard here—don't be alarmed if you see him. Better let you go now—I expect we'd all be grateful for a little sleep.'

XV

Holding the banister all the way to keep from falling backward or forward she crawled up steps going on forever and into her room. Here she pitched on the bed and lay for a timeless time unmoving. What came chiefly through her spinning annihilation was laughter, howls of obscene laughter; *they* stood out of sight in the wings laughing at the fool, the bad-luck fool who had dared to think her bad luck was over; the fool with her assumption, fatuous, of secure love and happiness. . . .

Worse than fool, dupe; a hurt more engulfing and destroying. But why, why . . . ? Feebly, eyeless in her fog, she wrestled with *why*. What element had it been, in the conspiracy between Myra and Tom . . .

A sickness plowed her violently and forced her to stop; she had to lie cancelled a moment, before resuming her hunt for the black cruelty hiding in blacker depths.

. . . what element, what heartlessness in their alliance had demanded the hoodwinking of their cat's-paw by a means so far-fetched as a proposal of marriage? what need to put her off her guard by a tactic so extreme, so unthinkable . . . ?

A calm overtook her, an access of cold sense. Myra had lied about being in his room, that was all. Obvious, how blatantly obvious; another of her fantastic lies, she was always lying . . .

She was in his room all right, he doesn't deny it.

The memory, echoing, struck her once more into the pit. No need either to exhaust herself finding an explanation, for the explanation—once one looked—was ludicrously simple. The old pattern, the old stale pattern, the man attractive, the woman stupid and trusting, lonely for love and cherishing. . . . Nor was this the first time she had taken on trust a beautiful exterior full of rottenness; still a goggle-eyed innocent, she had learned nothing from her first bad marriage.—Or perhaps by some lunatic caprice he had even meant his proposal, as a weak amiable man—in a moment of emotion—may say anything and believe what he says. Yet his way of looking at her; his voice, his arms, his kisses. . . . .

As she shrivelled with fierce self-loathing, with equal fierceness she began fighting for him again. It was all some frightful mistake, some grotesque misunderstanding. Impossible that his kindness and goodness should be a lie, that his gentleness, his considerateness and his ardour should all be a lie. . . .

She was in his room all right, he doesn't deny it.

The merciless hammer struck her down again; she lay sweating and panting. Then once more she roused herself to devise other reasons, excuses, explanations; she had to understand what had happened or she would go mad. What if the old affair he mentioned had been with Myra; nothing so terrible in that. What if, on the heels of his father's funeral, he should take refuge in the embrace of life; it was another of those ricochets that she herself had experienced in less violent form, when the news of death had sent her rushing off to buy new clothes. Or what if—even—his story of an affair long over were untrue, what if he had been sleeping with Myra all the while . . . nothing so terrible in that either, modern

thinking allowed for such things and she should be
civilized enough to go along with it. . . .

No use; however she looked at it she could see nothing
but such corruption that the thought of suicide began
to be purification, a cleansing escape from the filth of
betrayal. . . . She spared a last faint grimace for her
speculation on his hidden mistress, his far-away love,
when all the time the mistress had been no farther
away than Myra. Always the mug, the fool. . . . Parching
hot but shivering she groped for a corner of blanket,
pulled it up and lay under it, abandoned to the slow black
tide that washed her to and fro, to and fro, from waking
nightmare to sleeping nightmare. . . .

She was standing in a wasteland before a solitary tree
that reared up against a torn angry sunset, frightening.
But the tree itself was frightening, one straight barren
shaft going up and up to the clouds, where it split into
two thick bare arms reaching right and left; she had
never seen a tree of such terrifying unnatural height. The
tree started falling toward her; she stood directly in the
path of its fall, unable to move hand or foot. Slowly, inexorably it toppled toward her with a rending noise,
crackings first dull and then sharp, sharper, crack, crack,
crack . . .

She started from shallow sleep to the knocking at her
door, then floundered off the bed and went to open it.
Her old friend stood there, the inquisitor of the lounge.

'Miss Pendrell, please come with me at once.' His
voice, kept low, was peremptory. 'Hurry, will you, we've
no time to lose. I'll wait for you downstairs.'

As he disappeared she pivoted clumsily about, extorting haste from her clumsiness, and saw the new smart
hat leering at her like a skull. Groping for her umbrella
she hooked the old hat down off the press and crammed

it on anyhow. Then she picked up the utility camel's-hair, got one arm into it, and went downstairs on buckling legs; only her grip on the handrail saved her from falling bodily the last couple of steps.

'Steady,' said the Inspector, taking her arm, and hurried her out to the car, a massive shadow with staring yellow eyes. It was only as she got in that her padding feet reminded her that though fully dressed, she was still wearing bedroom slippers.

'Miss MacKinnon has asked for you,' he said urgently as they started moving—then paused, patently distrusting her staring disheveled look. 'Miss Pendrell! did you hear me?'

'Yes,' she said too loudly. 'Yes, I heard you. How—' her unmastered voice struck disagreeably on her ears; she tried to modulate it. '—how is Mrs. Lees-Milburn?'

His grunt, saturnine, was also a tribute.

'Talk about iron constitutions! Brimstone's more like it. D'you know what she said?' he demanded. 'Even in her condition? "She was in his room, the shameless guttersnipe." Believe it or not, she got that out.'

She felt nothing; the death in her was already accomplished.

'At least—' he was doleful again '—least it's confirmation.'

'And how is she—now?'

'Dead,' he returned. 'Within the last half-hour. Not from head injuries either, only from shock and loss of blood—tough old girl.—Now Miss Pendrell.' Again his voice had an exigency of steel. 'They don't expect Miss MacKinnon will recover either.'

He acknowledged her stupor of shock with another hard look, and pressed on. 'The charge is now murder or manslaughter, and one person remains to face it. So we've got to clear up Durant's part in it—his degree of implication.'

'Wh-what did you say?' she asked thickly.

'He's involved, don't you see?' he laid it out painstakingly, as if to an idiot. 'Her being in his room just before the incident involves—seems to involve—the two of them in whatever was going on. What that was we've yet to find out, but we shall. So get her to tell you where he comes into this.' He gave her another of those ruthless extorting looks. 'Steer the talk in that direction every way you know. It's important, never forget how important—in a capital charge like this.'

He let her digest it; out of a witless vertigo she managed finally, 'You mean . . . if Myra dies without saying what really happened, you mean that . . . that Mr. Durant . . . is left to face the whole charge alone?'

'What else?' he said brutally. 'We've got to establish his complicity in the events that led up to this business. There was a close association between the two of them, yes, but what was his *part* in it? So try and see if you can't make her talk about Durant,' he urged imperiously. 'Remember—!'

She said nothing, staring out of a window where only blackness was to be seen. All this was *not*, by shutting it away she could make it *not*; non-existent. Then a sort of earth-tremor had displaced her in time and space. Was this the same day or next day? Had she slept, fully dressed, through the whole next day till evening? In the sky was no testimony of dawn. In what segment of time did she now exist?

'Is it tomorrow?' she blurted.

'Tomorrow—?' Then with a short unamused bark he

understood her. 'No, Miss Pendrell, we talked less than two hours ago. It's not yet six—six of a dark morning.'

Reoriented, she wondered why she had wondered.

'There's a mike in the reading-light over her bed,' he was saying. 'Don't worry if she can only whisper—we'll get it.'

Bludgeoned to the lowest depths, as she thought, it was astonishing that he could find words to bludgeon her still lower.

'If she begins sinking, a sister'll come in and freshen her up,' he instructed sharply. 'Durant's position in this is the reason—the *only* reason—the hospital's cooperating to such an extent.'

Again she said nothing; they rode and rode through darkness. Yet in this trough of night was a runnel of darker night, that sucked and dragged at the flame of human vitality so that—according to doctors, was it?— most deaths took place between two and three in the morning . . . but this was not two or three, it was nearly six and pitch-black. Still, late November, and not six actually, not five o'clock . . . . with such dregs of thought one could stave off real thought, nothing mattered but keeping it at bay, keeping thought away at all costs. . . .

Myra acknowledged her entrance by opening her eyes slowly, yet immediately—then closing them again. Alison, noiseless on her slippered feet, padded to the chair beside the bed and sat down. A shell empty of thought, feeling or intention, for a mindless interval she tried to recognize the face on the pillow, feature by feature. Not Myra's pretty face, too small and too old, bloodless; not Myra's curving lips, now a faint grey line. Myra's neat and shapely nose, surely it had never been so pinched nor its bridge so sharp before, bone-sharp? But her hair was young and alive, the hair spread wavy and cloudy and dark on the white pillow. . . .

The silence went on and on; she made no least attempt to break it. She had promised nothing to that man out there, with his command to force a dying woman, compel her to talk . . . about . . .

Wildly she fled the name, pursued by a feeble gust of conscience. If she failed to make Myra talk he might be in the most terrible trouble . . . let him be, what difference to her, why strive for his benefit? Not that she hated him now, having died she was past loving or hating. Let him struggle by himself out of the quicksand where his treachery had led him. Also—a qualmish thought—what Myra had to say might involve him still more deeply; make the quicksand close over his head. . . . Terror lanced her so destructively that—with no idea what to say, with nothing in her but love for him and mortal fear on his behalf—she bent abruptly toward the bed, at the same instant that the woman in it opened her eyes again.

'Stupid,' breathed Myra, with a boundless yet shadowy despair. She took no notice of her visitor, but addressed herself to the farther wall. 'Stupid, stupid.' Having said it conclusively, her eyes again acknowledged the newcomer; she put out her hand, and Alison took and held it.

'Oh Bally,' sighed Myra. 'I'm so tired.'

She spoke clearly, yet always against intermittent failure of strength.

'Tired of lying,' she pursued gropingly. 'Pretending I'm important when I'm not—pretending I'm run after when I'm not.' She drew a shaky breath. 'Stupid, all so stupid . . . isn't it, Bally? Isn't it?'

Her voice died; an aura of collapse seemed to efface her. At that instant a sister entered swiftly and bent over the bed. When she straightened some moments later Myra lay motionless, again with eyes closed.

'Give it a minute,' the sister mouthed in Alison's ear almost inaudibly. 'To take hold.' She retreated slightly and beckoned; when Alison shook her head at the invitation to follow, she bent down again and whispered imperiously, 'You're not trying, the Inspector says. You must *help* her talk, suggest things, give her a lead,' and for answer got full in her face a look of such Medusa-like repulse that she drew back hastily and left.

Silence descended again like a snowfall; in the watcher began stirring an unwilled urgency of panic. Myra lay there with her secrets, in a few moments she might be past speaking and it would be too late, forever too late. . . . *So let him get out of it himself*, she thought again stridently, yet began fumbling more and more desperately for a first question, elicit from Myra what only Myra could tell. . . . Fascinated, she saw a faint aliveness reanimating the face, a faint clarity and firmness of outline. Now, now, try now. . . .

'Oh Bally,' Myra cut her off. Her eyes were open again, her voice—perceptibly stronger—was yet a moan of despair. 'Oh God I loved him, I loved him so. Oh Tom, Tom. . . .' The thread of voice frayed, recovered, went on spinning its lamentation. 'All these years I loved him, Oh God it was awful, awful . . . . and he so *nice* to me, damn him, so polite . . . I wasn't alive, for him, I was an item of staff, useful . . .'

She stared back along some unseen and stricken vista. 'And then . . . and then . . .'

Holding Myra's hand more closely, Alison crouched nearer the bed. A vertigo of hope swung her in nauseating circles; she dared believe in it no more than she dared breathe. In this vacuum where she hung suspended, hope given entrance and then blasted was a culminating death to the deaths she had already undergone.

'It was . . . after his father's funeral. He'd been away for days—and came back very late last night, Sunday night.'

Like herself, Alison thought vaguely; they must have missed each other by the least margin, only by moments.

'. . . and all at once I couldn't bear it any more, I couldn't bear it. I thought, now that he's alone and sad . . . now, now, if in this moment he knew that—that close by—there was someone who loved him Oh with . . . with all her heart, someone . . .'

Her eyes were wide, appalled.

'. . . so I just went to his room. I was ready to die of fright but I wouldn't let myself think, I didn't care, I was walking outside myself, I . . . nothing mattered, I couldn't help. . . . I had to see him, *see* him . . .'

A change came over her, least to be expected; in all her terrible weakness, a composure and coldness.

'His door wasn't locked—I just turned the knob and went in. He hadn't even begun undressing, he was just sitting there.' Her voice was now hard and dispassionate, hardly faltering at all. 'I don't remember that I said any-thing—just reached out my arms. And he—'

An intake of breath, rasping, halted her for a full moment.

'—he just got up and put me out. Without a wasted word—or motion. Efficient.' She smiled horribly. 'Not rough, you know, very gentle actually. I think he said *My dear Miss MacKinnon, now really,* something like that. Embarrassed I expect but he didn't show it—sorry for me too probably, but I was a . . . just a nuisance to be dealt with, quickly—got rid of. The whole thing took about . . . two seconds.'

She paused again.

'He put me—*out*. And no one that saw could miss it—that I'd been shoved out. *She* didn't miss it.'

The smile of undiminished hatred in the diminished face was chilling.

'She was in the hall, damn her soul—on her way to unship her rotten old kidneys, I expect. And happened to be standing—exactly right—to see what had been done to me. You can't mistake . . . eviction.' She drew breath painfully. 'Old bitch from hell standing there and grinning at me—with her three or four long yellow fangs she's got left. Well, I was . . . paralyzed, of course. And she walked up to me and said, "Tomorrow morning, everyone in this house will know."'

On a long sigh she stopped dead, closing her eyes, yet opened them almost at once.

'And I lost my head—completely.' The unnatural composure of her voice was now, if anything, reinforced. 'All I could think of was—being slung out of Mowbray's . . . being completely at that old hag's mercy . . . and before I could think I'd blurted out, "Oh please don't tell, please."—*That's* what I can't bear—that I grovelled to her.' Myra gritted her teeth weakly. 'And of course—she laughed in my face. And Bally, Bally—' it was sheerest supplication '—I didn't mind her laughing, Oh I didn't, what else could I expect. But then—but then—'

Once more she stopped dead, differently from the other times; nerving herself to the unbearable.

'—then she said, "Went to his room did you, you nasty slut, threw yourself at his head? And he—" and *laughing*, Bally, she was laughing all the while "—and he wouldn't touch you with a pair of tongs, not he." And that—that tore it.' She gulped and began talking faster. 'I picked up one of those vases and went for her. And she . . . *screamed* . . . and began running. Afraid, for one moment she was afraid. Does me good.' Enjoyment lit her, a baleful flicker. 'And don't think I was out of my head, I wasn't. I wanted to kill her and I tried to kill her, the best I knew—' she checked. 'How is she?'

'Dead,' said Alison. 'About an hour ago.'

'Good,' said Myra. 'Evil . . . evil old scrag. But when—when I saw her fall—' a new wavering took her, destructive '—one thought, just one, flashed across me. *He's destroyed me—I'll destroy him.* So I told it that way—I pulled him into it. I knew I was going to end it straightaway, get myself right out of it—and he'd be in it alone, up to the neck. And it would hurt him . . . a lot. Even if he cleared himself there'd be a noise about it, publicity. . . . Bally.' Her hand in Alison's tightened weakly. 'Bally, where is he now?'

'I've not seen him,' Alison murmured.

'But they . . . they'd have taken him? away?'

'Yes, they must have done.'

'Has anyone—mentioned Tom? at all?'

'Yes, that officer.'

'What?' a voice demanded out of torment. 'What did he say?'

'Just that he was involved.'

'But—but didn't the man tell you what Tom had said? Nothing at all—?'

'Nothing at all, except,' Alison returned slowly, 'that he's refusing to say anything whatever.'

Across Myra's face flashed a scorn unmistakable but enigmatic. While Alison still gaped at it, uncomprehending, the girl in the bed dozed suddenly—an appearance contradicted almost at once by her opening eyes. 'Don't go, Bally,' she entreated. 'I'm not tired—don't go.'

'I shan't go,' Alison soothed. Her heartbroken inward weeping must be concealed at all costs lest Myra, fiendishly intuitive, should know it for what it was—pity—and thrust it back with mortal resentment. 'Of course I shan't go.'

'I wasn't going to tell anyone—what I did to him. To Tom.' Myra was plumbing weakly some unknown shadowy depth. 'But I couldn't just leave him in it like that, too beastly—I had to tell. Not to a stranger.' Her forlornness became more forlorn. 'It wasn't so bad, telling you. You're my friend.'

'Oh yes, Myra,' Alison returned. 'Oh yes, yes.'

'That foul old woman making . . . trouble . . . between us,' Myra strove. 'It didn't . . . count.'

'Not ever,' Alison affirmed. 'It didn't count,' then through unwilled extremity blurted, 'But why didn't Mr. Durant *tell* them? why didn't he just tell them what happened—' then stopped as suddenly as she had started, with incredulity realizing her trespass of curiosity upon what moment. 'No, no, never mind, I didn't mean—'

'Men,' Myra said with astonishing clarity, cutting across her. Her scorn, deep before, was consuming. 'A man do anything so simple . . . or sensible?'

Smiling darkly and secretly, pausing often, she struggled on with undiminished contempt.

'Bad. It looked bad for him. Whatever he'd say, they'd suspect him. Deny . . . any man'd deny it, they'd expect him to. So he'd rather wait for his solicitor before he . . . got 'mself in deep. Pairfec'ly sensible. But that's not . . . all.'

She paused, gathering herself.

'*Afraid,*' she breathed. 'A man—putting a woman out

of his room? defending 's virtue? Look a . . . a fool, won'
he?' Along with a faint return of her childhood accent
she had begun slurring words, dropping syllables, saving
strength and breath. 'So rather'n look ridic'lous he'd let
them . . . arrest . . .' The amusement in her face grew
darker.

'Men—all the same. Sell their souls—ev'ry time—t'save
their conceit. Call it their . . . pride. Get hold of things
—by the wrong end—ev'ry time.'

In her sinking look was a wan incandescence of hatred.
'Men,' she murmured. '*Men.*'

A drowsiness had extinguished her moments ago, yet
the sleep in her face was not final sleep, not yet. In the
void of waiting, the void of complete self-abnegation,
Alison attended as if upon a summons. With head downbent her eyes traced and retraced the weave of the same
square inch of hospital bed linen as if it held the solution
of some profound mystery. Nothing existed but the pattern of threads, and the waiting, and Myra's small cold
hand that she now held in both her own. Vaguely at last
it seemed to her that this hand, without moving at all,
was somehow withdrawing from her own, getting
smaller. . . . Frightened, she looked up to find Myra's
eyes fixed steadily upon her—with such a curious half-
smile that she started guiltily. What had betrayed her,
what passing of despair from her face, what renewal of
life, she was not to know then or later.

Averting her glance too quickly with consternation,
and returning it too quickly with consternation, to her
own horror she felt a burning in her cheeks and could
guess from it her burning colour. Myra's smile—so different from those other hating contemptuous smiles—
deepened; out of her receding face there glinted not

only Myra's deadly intuition, but the Myra of long ago; the young Myra of bright hopes not yet tarnished with disappointment, of bright mischief not yet cankered with heartsickness and malice. As if in answer to her friend's imprisoned stare she murmured, 'Mister Durant, did you call him?'

She made a small sound, desolation itself and yet a laugh.

'Bally.' Just only able to, she raised her hand and beckoned. 'Bally . . .'

Alison bent close to catch the failing whisper, in whose mockery walked the ghost of an old affection and good-will.

'Bally, you know what? I just saw . . . the Fourth Man . . . climb off your back.'